The
Stories

Amazing Beasts

Edited By Andy Porter

First published in Great Britain in 2022 by:

**YoungWriters®** Est. 1991

Young Writers
Remus House
Coltsfoot Drive
Peterborough
PE2 9BF
Telephone: 01733 890066
Website: www.youngwriters.co.uk

Printed and bound in the UK by BookPrintingUK
Website: www.bookprintinguk.com
YB0512E

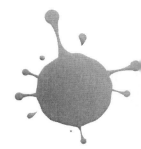

Foreword

Welcome Reader!

Are you ready to discover strange and wonderful creatures that you'd never even dreamed of?

For Young Writers' latest competition 'Bonkers Monsters', we asked primary school pupils to create a creature of their own invention, and then write a story about it using just 100 words - a hard task! However, they rose to the challenge magnificently and the result is this fantastic collection full of creepy critters and amazing animals!

Here at Young Writers our aim is to encourage creativity in children and to inspire a love of the written word, so it's great to get such an amazing response, with some absolutely fantastic stories.

Not only have these young authors created imaginative and inventive monsters, they've also crafted wonderful tales to showcase their creations. These stories are brimming with inspiration and cover a wide range of themes and emotions - from fun to fear and back again!

I'd like to congratulate all the young authors in this anthology, I hope this inspires them to continue with their creative writing.

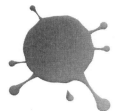

Contents

Calvin Cormack (9)	63
Mark Griffiths (9)	64
Blaire Robertson (9)	65
Saphia Clement (9)	66
Matthew Allen (9)	67
Amy Weir (9)	68
Sofia Wells (9)	69
Rion Watson (9)	70
Olivia Labus (9)	71
Katie Murray (9)	72
Abigail Dowding (9)	73

Fane Street Primary School, Belfast

Rosha Mohammadi (8)	74
Ahmed Ahmed (9)	75
Kieran Jiang (9)	76
Dylan McConville (9)	77

Godstone Primary & Nursery School, Godstone

Verity Nicholson (9)	78
Merry Thackray (10)	79
Jess Young (10)	80
Francesca Roberts (10)	81
Antonio Pini (10)	82
Millie Hoare-Simpson (10)	83
Beritan Buyukertas (10)	84
Jessica Biggs (10)	85
Lois Spencer (10)	86
Evie Bradley (9)	87
Eleanor Scott (10)	88
Amelia Bateman (10)	89
Joshua Farrow (10)	90
Riley Snashfold (10)	91
Izzy Mosley (10)	92
Noah Austin (9)	93
Alexander Mathews (9)	94
Ollie Chiappa (9)	95
Alannah Sheehan (10)	96
Evie Norman (9)	97
Jacob Crozier (9)	98

Gorebridge Primary School, Gorebridge

Riley Demirtas (11)	99
David Simpson (11)	100
Finlay Phillips (11)	101
Sam Jameson (11)	102
Aaron K (11)	103
Kaitlyn Black (11)	104
Skye Stevenson (11)	105

High Green Primary School, High Green

Phoebe Green (8)	106
Isabelle Gamban (7)	107
Frank Parkinson (7)	108
Georgiana Webster (7)	109
Sophia Stupple (8)	110
Imogen Eeles (8)	111
Georgia Streets (8)	112
Layla Hill (8)	113
Elsie Richardson (7)	114
Casey Cottam (7)	115

Kingston St Mary CE (VC) Primary School, Kingston St Mary

Maeve Platts (6)	116
William Sweeting (7)	117
Edith House (7)	118
Harry Bewes (7)	119
Clara O'Keeffe (6)	120
Jake Ewing (7)	121
Jack Gray (7)	122
Dolly-Rae Sharland (6)	123
Alex Parkinson (7)	124
Jacob Glynn (7)	125
Sophia Tompkins (6)	126
Phoebe Cann (6)	127
Connie Mace (7)	128
Stanley Hartnell (7)	129
Scarlett Goretzka (7)	130
Hunter Forrest	131

Sasha Peckitt (7) — 132
Harry Morgan (7) — 133
Charlie Hull (7) — 134

Moorland Primary School, Beanhill

Bushra Ahmed (7) — 135
Ella Ogunkoya (7) — 136
Anna Rzepecka (9) — 137
Olivia DeRoche (8) — 138
Fatimah Abdul Kader (8) — 139
Janice Zira (8) — 140
Dexter Mardel (10) — 141
Reuben Greenall (10) — 142
Kya Durman (10) — 143
Quincy Zira (10) — 144
Connor Lacey (7) — 145
Sumayyah Kigozi (7) — 146
Hassan Naqvi (6) — 147
Dara Olorode (6) — 148
Isla Bickerdike (6) — 149
Ruth Boakye (6) — 150
Oli Patton (6) — 151
Destiny Edwards (11) — 152

Our Lady Of Lourdes Catholic Primary School, Birkdale

Lucy Antrobus — 153
Madison Fashoni (10) — 154
Daisy Halfpenny (10) — 155
Sean Porter (9) — 156
Emilia Gregoriou (10) — 157
Jack Higham (10) — 158
Sienna Shawcroft (9) — 159
Matilda Hunter-Wearing (9) — 160
Noah Gavan (9) — 161
Seve Arthur (10) — 162
Alfie Owens (9) — 163
Lily Friel (10) — 164
Emilia Gorna (9) — 165
Emma Moreno Gouveia (10) — 166
Louisa Lunn-Bates (9) — 167

Edward Halsall (10) — 168

Priory School, Slough

Rida Fathima (10) — 169
Eesa Khan (7) — 170
Zayn Ahmed (8) — 171
Evie Prescott (9) — 172
Mishika Ahluwa Lia (9) — 173
Ruby Gill (8) — 174
Saiuri K Naidu (9) — 175
Vihaan Panchal (7) — 176
Nafisa Khan (9) — 177
Yasmin Zekari-Day (10) — 178
Esha Tandon (10) — 179
Abdullah Basit (7) — 180
Hasan Jawad (10) — 181

Vita Et Pax Preparatory School, Southgate

Alana Chan (7) — 182
Martyn Yavari (7) — 183
Emilia Maestri (6) — 184
Francesca Spiteri (7) — 185
Ellena Wilson (7) — 186
Emily Strien (6) — 187
Joseph Murphy (7) — 188
Hannah Vallayil (5) — 189

The Monster House

Deep in the dark, cold woods, the trees were swaying, the wind was howling. Three children went on an adventure.

"Stop!" shouted Mabel. "We need to go home now."

"Not yet, look what I found," said Terrance.

In the distance was a colourful house standing alone.

"I can hear music."

The children ran towards the house. It was open. To their surprise, they saw a three-legged, green, fluffy monster dancing and singing with some of his monster friends.

"We are family," Sillybut sang. "Come and join the party," he said.

The children danced and sang all night.

Gracie-Louise Turner (7)

Bentley St Paul's CE (VA) Primary School, Bentley

The Monster TD

Once, there was a monster named TD. He was smart, clever and kind. He loved making new friends. Every day after school, he would race home, eat as fast as he could and then he'd race to his favourite place in the world at around 3:45pm. He'd eat dinner, and he would call his friends. One day after school, he went to the park. He saw a goblin who was ripping the flowers. The monster said, "That's not right!"
Goblin said, "Yes, it is because I'm not beautiful."
"You can be kind every day and like this you are beautiful."
"Sure."

Teo Petre (8)
Bentley St Paul's CE (VA) Primary School, Bentley

Bakon

Bakon was a monster. Like any other monster, really. He walked, talked just like a monster. But there was something different about him. Something extraordinary. His name. Bacon is normally with a 'c' but his was a 'k'! And just because of that, people bullied him. Mocked him. Even though he just wanted to make the world a better place. He had a campaign for becoming the next president of Monster Land. The polls were in and he won! Even though nobody cheered, he felt proud. It was time for a speech. And he only said two words: "Be yourself."

Ope Davids (11)
Bentley St Paul's CE (VA) Primary School, Bentley

Fluffball And Chick

Fluffball was a monster but not a mean one. He was a cute, fluffy, kind one. He brought toys to life. Anyone, elephants to bears to giraffes. And he played with all of the toys.

One night, Fluffball was feeling lonely so he crept inside a house and brought a cute, fuzzy chick to life. He played with Chick all night long, they laughed and jumped about together.

Soon, it was morning and the chick froze again. He jumped out the window, full of happiness. Fluffball snuggled up in his warm, cosy, lovely, furry, rainbow and silver-black bed and slept.

Elisa Chambrier (9)
Bentley St Paul's CE (VA) Primary School, Bentley

Blobtipus The Saviour

Once upon a time, there was this freak called Blobtipus. He had eight legs like an octopus. When he was flying for fun, he saw a girl in trouble who was getting bullied by his enemy, Trod.

He lunged, came up to Trod and said, "Pick on someone your own size!"

Trod laughed at him and said, "What are you going to do about it?"

Blobtipus said, "This," and he punched him and knocked him out.

Then he flew the girl to his cave in the sea, gave her scuba gear and said, "Now we can see each other more."

Matthew Malatsi (8)

Bentley St Paul's CE (VA) Primary School, Bentley

Cosmo's Crazy Haircut!

Cosmo was a horrifically hairy monster. He had a busy, bossy dream of getting his long, green, wild hair cut. One grey, rainy day, Cosmo had nothing to do. Then, he had a great idea! He would go to the hair salon. Nobody was there, so Cosmo went crazy. He squirted shampoo all over the mirrors and found a pair of sharp, silver scissors. Cosmo began chopping his hair so he could look as good as new. Suddenly, footsteps approached. Cosmo jumped to his three-toed feet and scrambled as fast as fury, back to his cave. He loved his new haircut!

Holly Warner (7)
Bentley St Paul's CE (VA) Primary School, Bentley

Swamp Monster

Gerald was a green, scary-looking monster, who lived in a green, slimy, bogey-like swamp; no friends and a really poopy smell were all he knew. One day, Gerald decided to leave the swamp and find some friends. He slithered out of the swamp, but every creature or person he met screamed and ran away. Gerald decided he would be happier if he was not so smelly. Quietly, and after dark, he made his way to the sea. Once in the water, all the smelly poo washed off and Gerald looked sparkly clean. Gerald made friends with a joyful shark!

Samuel Wilkinson (8)
Bentley St Paul's CE (VA) Primary School, Bentley

Lolo And The Stranger

As I ran away from the searchlights, I hid behind a tree. I waited until I couldn't hear them anymore and made my way out of the forest. I soon came to a village, a bit like my one at home. I climbed through one of the house's open windows and looked around. Just then, I accidentally knocked over a plate and almost at once someone came in! I quickly dashed behind a counter but the human still found me! At first, I thought he would scream, but he just smiled and said, "Let's get you home, shall we?"

Alice Scott (10)
Bentley St Paul's CE (VA) Primary School, Bentley

Moon Mud

One day, Moon Mud the monster was adventuring through the woods and he bumped into a fox. The fox was very angry and took Moon Mud to his den. A badger let Moon Mud the monster free. Moon Mud saw a horse and jumped on the horse's back. He was horse-riding. Moon Mud saw other horses, so he jumped on one of the other horses. More monsters came, they all jumped on horses and had a party.

Grace Holdgate (7)
Bentley St Paul's CE (VA) Primary School, Bentley

Scritch-Scratch's New Home!

Once upon a time, there lived a monster called Scritch-Scratch. One day, Scritch-Scratch went to Planet Bong. It was quite boring, but suddenly Planet Bong was a place of wonder, there were games and friends and Scritch-Scratch played tag a lot. It was amazing! He loved being on Planet Bong and his friends loved him even more! They all lived happily ever after.

Cara Evans (7)
Bentley St Paul's CE (VA) Primary School, Bentley

Huggie Wuggie

One day, a child went to a toy store and he saw Huggie Wuggie on a stand. Then Huggie Wuggie came to life and started playing with the child. Then they had a disco, and then Huggie Wuggie tucked the kid in bed and said, "Good night." The next morning, Huggie Wuggie made pancakes for the kid.

Tommy Cook-Smith (6)
Bentley St Paul's CE (VA) Primary School, Bentley

Equal Rights For All!

Crash! A ship crash-landed on Planet Senas.
"Ooh!" said Pickle, a curious monster.
Suddenly, a monster came out of it, followed by many others.
"I'm so sorry!" began the monster.
Monsters started shouting, "Oi," "Out," and "What do you think you're doing?"
Pickle stepped in.
"These people are new, what's so wrong?"
"Everything!"
Pickle was shocked. She started shouting out that this was wrong! Two weeks later, she said that this had happened on Earth and would not happen here. Monsters agreed with her. Soon, everyone agreed. Everyone liked each other.
"Happy days!" shouted Pickle and her friends.

Felix Barnett (8)
Dulwich Hamlet Junior School, London

12

The Magic Of Dust

Staring at the midnight sky, Zepandapeng saw sparkling spirit dust swirling around the crescent moon.

"Why can others not see the spirits of the night?" Mysteriously, Zepandapeng's alethiometer symbols had faded recently. A thought crossed the creature's mind. Sprinkle dust over it and magic might happen. Zepandapeng grabbed the golden compass and launched it into the air. Immediately, a face appeared on the moon.

Unafraid, Zepandapeng listened; "You are special. Your alethiometer lost its illustrations because you doubted yourself. Everyone has a gift. Keep your spirits up. Time will tell."

With that, the alethiometer's pictures appeared and the figure vanished.

Hattie Hollands (8)
Dulwich Hamlet Junior School, London

The Last Goodbye

Molly stood, staring at the wrecked ground where her sister's last resting place was. The stone was cracked, and any flowers were ripped to shreds. She watched as silently, two skeletal hands reached the surface. Then a skull emerged with the rest of the body.

"Jenny?" Molly asked, "What's wrong?"

All that escaped from Jenny's mouth was a moan. But it meant something. Molly knew. Jenny tried again, and now it worked.

"Never got to say g-goodbye..." she croaked.

"Oh Jen, I'm so sorry."

Jenny smiled and stepped forwards, arms outstretched.

Then, as she fell, she whispered, "I love you."

Rosita Esslemont (11)
Dulwich Hamlet Junior School, London

14

Dodo Ba And Peep

One day, Peep was walking. Suddenly, a hairy arm reached out and grabbed Peep. Peep screamed. The monster's name was Dodo Ba. He was mean and tough. He took Peep to his lair. At night, Peep had an idea.

So when it was eight o'clock, Peep woke up and said, "Hey Dodo Ba."

"What?"

"Why don't we have a race on ice?"

"Okay."

"Okay."

Pew, pew, pew, pew. Finally, finished!

"I won, yay, go me, go me!"

"Oh, uh, good job."

"Bye Dodo Ba."

"Bye Peep."

"Yay! I'm free!"

Zora Bakic Gazibara (8)
Dulwich Hamlet Junior School, London

May The Upstander

At monster school, May was bullied for wearing glasses on her three eyes.

"Freakshow! Normal monsters have one eye!" they said.

She ran into the forest, crying. The day faded, owls hooted and May was scared. Suddenly, she saw light from a camp with a glowing fire. A silhouetted figure asked May softly why she was there.

She replied, "I couldn't take the bullying anymore."

"You can't change what you look like," he said, "but you can change how you feel about yourself." He guided May back to school. The bullies came but May just smiled. She wasn't afraid now.

Ivy Vulkan (8)
Dulwich Hamlet Junior School, London

Chaotic Midnight Feasts And More!

The fair was in full flow and it was approaching midnight. Then, suddenly, the lights went out. When they came back on, Destiny and her bluebird friends had disappeared! Bangolina felt a tingle in her magical crystal - the future started to appear. "Donenyea's luring the bluebirds!" she shouted. "What shall we do to get them back?" a little Mouset screamed.
"Candyfloss!"
The candyfloss owner started spinning a huge ball and Bangolina tied it to string, pulled the end and flew. One bluebird appeared, then the sky was filled with them and everyone let out a great, big cheer!

Leila Meryon (8)
Dulwich Hamlet Junior School, London

A Fright In The Night?

Derek was collecting wood from the forest. The forest was dark and dense and it had that cold and menacing feeling, especially tonight as there was a storm. The winds were wild and the rain was pouring down, it was deadly. Derek zipped up his jacket and jumped out from behind a tree. A monster thought he was playing hide-and-seek so he joined in.

"Boo!" he exclaimed.

Derek turned. He looked. Friendly eyes were staring at him and a smile.

"Oh, we're playing?" said Derek.

"Would you like to play?" asked the monster.

Derek smiled and nodded.

"Yes!"

Molly DCG (8)

Dulwich Hamlet Junior School, London

The Slime

Once upon a time, there was a nice, beautiful monster called Monty who loved Skittles. One day, he saw a trail of Skittles and followed it. It finished outside.

"Mmm," said Monty.

Monty looked up and saw the Slime Guy! Oh no, he was back! Then Monty realised he could spit out weapons. Monty spat and out came a sword.

"Go away!" shouted Monty, "Go away!" he repeated.

Slime Guy was so scared that he ran away.

"Yay!" everyone screamed.

After that, everyone had an enormous, grand party. Everyone was having fun. Monty was a hero who lived good days!

Lucia Gimenez-Zapiola (9)
Dulwich Hamlet Junior School, London

The Salty Swamp

Dripping luminous green slime, a shape-shifting monster emerged from the bubbling swamp. It showed its sharp teeth and slobbered on the forest floor. The first person to see the horrifying monster was Tom. He screamed for his family. The monster slurped towards him. He backed away. The tent they'd camped in was next to Tom. He grabbed a fishing net and squashed it hard over the approaching monster. Thousands of slippery swamplings spawned from the net's holes, sliding around like slugs. Tom snatched the picnic supplies and threw salt all over them. They quickly shrivelled to dry, dead crusts.

Fred Newman (8)
Dulwich Hamlet Junior School, London

Teenager Tantrum

Katie was Astrid's only friend. Upon Halls, in the Sixth Form building, a short girl, who was too small for her locker was shouted at, being called a monster for you know what reason. In class, she thought of ways to stop this happening. In the grounds, she set up a stall and protested against name-calling. Nobody came. Then she had an idea. Give them a taste of their own medicine!
So out she called, "Hey monster!"
Everyone stared. She knew all their weaknesses.
"Did I mention I was called monster?"
Laughing, Katie was there. "That felt good!"

Zoe Coughlan (7)
Dulwich Hamlet Junior School, London

The Keeper Of The Dead

In the boiling magma of Death Volcano lay the evil, bloodthirsty Keeper of the Dead. Meanwhile, in the Village of Happiness, people were sleeping in the village hall, not knowing they would regret their midnight slumber. Slowly, quietly, the creature woke up, smelling human flesh. With a big crash, the hall door collapsed, revealing six bloodshot eyes. In the blink of an eye, there was nothing left but bloody gore. The next morning, three heroes set out to kill the Keeper of the Dead. They fought heroically until the monster was slaughtered. Everyone lived happily ever after... or did they?

Oscar Arens (8)
Dulwich Hamlet Junior School, London

The Vampire And The Humans

There once was a vampire that lived happily, but then humans started to kill vampires, so then she would have to live with the humans. The humans knew that she was a vampire, so they hid Jess' fangs so they could put Jess into school.

Jess said, "Mum, I don't want to go to school. What if my fangs go out?"

"Don't worry, the principal knows that you're a vampire so don't worry," said the mum.

When Jess went to school, everyone knew that she was a vampire. They went on the school trip and then they stopped hating vampires.

Michelle Braga (7)
Dulwich Hamlet Junior School, London

Slimy Mcsnail Hater And The Suspicious Noise

As the mist shrouded over the craggy mountain, a peculiar-looking beast halted. He heard a deafening shriek in the distance. It sounded like someone needed help. He trundled onwards to the unfamiliar sound. From the corner of his eye, he spotted a lonely snail. He despised snails. They were his ultimate fear, especially slimy, grotesque snails. He sprinted as it emerged out of its shell. He stopped abruptly as he heard the sound coming from behind the log. He pried the log onto its side and there, etched with slime on the damp soil, read: 'Run For Your Life'.

Aaryan Acharya (9)
Dulwich Hamlet Junior School, London

Tu-Morrow

Once upon a time, there was a monster called Tu-morrow and she loved the market.

But one day, Per-fect said, "You are a horrible beast, stay away."

Tu-morrow did not like that, she did not like it one bit.

So she decided to say, "I am not going to listen to you anymore, you just say mean things."

And all of the other people said, "Just because she is a Bonkers Monster doesn't mean she is cruel like you!"

And so that was how the whole town became friends with Tu-morrow. Even Per-fect tried to join in.

Cydney Kellett-Cooper (10)
Dulwich Hamlet Junior School, London

In A Pickle

Skittish feet hopped along the floor. How I'd let this leathery, dark creature into my room, I didn't know, but this top hat wearing pickle seemed in no hurry to leave. In the past hours it had: smashed my lamp, ripped my sheets and crushed my desk. I'd hidden in my wardrobe, watching. Then, without warning, it scampered out and down the stairs. I ran, following its ugly scent. In a burst of courage, I flung a blanket around it and let Pickle stumble. Cold feet scraped the floor, a black shape flew past my parents, fading into the television...

Bea Newman (10)
Dulwich Hamlet Junior School, London

Rubble And The Polluted Planet

Rubble was skipping through the middle of the Earth when he stumbled upon a picnic. Suddenly, Rubble got hit on the bottom with a plastic bottle! He was furious, so he marched towards the Litter Bugs. There were chocolate wrappers everywhere and it made him melancholy. At that moment, one of the Litter Bugs skidded on a banana skin. Rubble helped the Litter Bug up and comforted him. All of the others were shocked by the incredible kindness. Finally, they felt guilty, so they started to pick up their rubbish and nobody ever threw trash on the floor again!

Lola Cicala (7)
Dulwich Hamlet Junior School, London

King Archery And The Beast

Once upon a nightmare, there lived a great king that would look after his people, a king that would hover over his kingdom like a hawk, a king named Archery. He was named this because his father loved archery. One Easter, they were gathered around a table, laughing and drinking beer. Around the corner, a hideous, bloodthirsty beast was planning her feast. The king, upon hearing this, decided to learn about her and defend his people. He challenged the beast to an almighty battle. After two hard days, the courageous king victoriously celebrated as a hero.

Breyelle David (9)
Dulwich Hamlet Junior School, London

Bug Crusher

In an underground hideout, a monster rose to the ground and surprised a boy. They walked together, stepping on many bugs on the way. This monster was called Sarpnos, he *hated* bugs! Stepping on a hundred more bugs, he met his match. A bug the same size as him blocked his way. He fought him but he was too strong. Sarpnos froze all the bugs around him. Without the bug noticing, Sarpnos turned into an elephant, but then a ladybird came and froze him. "Hooray for the ladybird!" That night there was a festival for all the bugs. Hooray!

Isabel Mingay (8)
Dulwich Hamlet Junior School, London

The Cavernous Caves And The Nameless North

Mia watched the cave, curious, with her back to the very thing that may kill her. She swivelled around and faced the monster. Shadow Mist's black cape circled around her entire body until she was covered, gone into wind. That wasn't the end though, as she fought back. Mia screamed as the monster gripped her tighter. She reached deep into her pocket for the blade and cut it in Mist's throat, which travelled past. But the power she used was enough to enable his heart to crack to pieces. Then gone, like the mist. Nothing, nothing was left.

Lucia Carpenter (9)
Dulwich Hamlet Junior School, London

The Lonely Monster

Once upon a time, there was a lonely little monster called Zog. He didn't have any friends at school, but one day, Zog's teacher, Mr Monzie, planned a special treat for 3M, to go to the Monster Museum. After the slime activity, they all sat down for lunch. Suddenly, Zog realised that he had forgotten his green, slimy sandwiches. He had a monster tear coming down his cheek. Luckily, a friendly monster called Zig came over and gave him a packet of delicious Monster Crunch and Zog stopped crying and was happy because he had a new friend.

Beatrice Hatherall (8)

Dulwich Hamlet Junior School, London

A Deep, Dark Fear

One bright morning, Tiny the monster from Planet Xyzkwhpsz was juggling some balls while thinking about bedtime because she was scared of the dark. She didn't want to admit it because she was worried someone would laugh at her. At bedtime, she would shiver and shake in her bed. She wanted to do something about it but she couldn't build up the courage to say it out loud, so it kept on going until she couldn't stand it anymore and she told her mum about it. Her mum said it didn't matter and that was the end to Tiny's fear!

Eva Gee (8)
Dulwich Hamlet Junior School, London

The Three-Eyed Monster

Once upon a time, there was an enormous monster with three eyes. The monster needed glasses, but the nearest optician only had glasses for two-eyed monsters. What to do? He tried some on in the shop but it was a disaster. The first pair was too tiny and fell off his head, the second pair covered his entire head. *I know*, he thought, *I'll make my own.* He bought two pairs of regular glasses and cut one in half, sticking them together. He now had a pair of three-eyed glasses. He was very excited. They were a perfect fit.

Max Rippe (7)
Dulwich Hamlet Junior School, London

Travelling Time!

Hi there, I am Banger and I love being in the USA. I am packing up to go to the UK. I am in my car now. I am almost at the airport, five minutes left. Okay. Let's go to the plane now. I am on the plane now. I can watch videos. Wait! I can see the Earth so close! Is that meant to happen?

"Argh! Help! Please!"

Boom! Where am I?

"Can I help you to fix the plane?"

"Yes, please. We need help to fix the plane."

"So that goes like that. Done."

To the UK now!

Aliona Kosheleva (8)

Dulwich Hamlet Junior School, London

Blobby And Amilia's Adventures On Earth!

There once lived an alien called Blobby and his friend called Amilia. They lived in a place called Blob Land in a universe far away. One day, they were walking down the road, Blobby spotted a portal! A bike was coming out, it knocked over Blobby. He fell in and dragged Amilia with him. They ended up on our planet, Earth. Luckily, a nice boy and his dog helped them build a portal in his shed. Meanwhile, on Blob Land, Blobby and Amilia's mums were all worried. Their children were gone! But a day later, they were back home, safe.

Florence Rigby (8)
Dulwich Hamlet Junior School, London

The Legend Of Rex

One day, a monster called Rex emerged. Some people say that he lives in the Iceland mountains, others say he is no longer alive. Rex saw in the distance there was an odd-looking creature struggling to get to the shore. Rex dived in lightning-fast to save him. He noticed that he was a human boy. The boy whispered to Rex that his mum and dad were up the Mountain of Hope. Rex mumbled to himself, "Should I help? Of course!"
On his way, there were many obstacles to face, but he succeeded in finding his mum and dad.

Sebastian Cuevas (8)
Dulwich Hamlet Junior School, London

Relba, Poppy And The Three Bullies!

A girl called Poppy lived with her mummy, Amy. Poppy was a happy girl, especially when she found a monster! She named her Relba. Poppy was bullied by a girl and two boys named Luanne, Alfie and George. One particular day, Poppy was in her room discussing how to scare away the bullies, which was quite easy because they had never seen Relba. So the next day, Relba hid behind a tree as the bullies were coming past and, "*Boo!*"
They ran away screaming! Luanne and George moved house. Alfie moved to Australia!

Sophia Couldrey (8)
Dulwich Hamlet Junior School, London

The Explosion Of People

Once in Book World, a book read ten books a day. He loved reading every book. When he read, his brain got bigger, bigger and bigger. He thought about what to do in beautiful, peaceful Book World when the book stumbled upon a swirly, black thing. He hopped in. In the monstrous place he saw humans, he said hi but everyone ran. With nothing to do, he went to an unused room and pulled bombs out of him. He went to destroy every city. In Belgium, everyone threw waffles and chocolate. He got dropped in England. Everyone was blown up.

Coleman Mears (8)
Dulwich Hamlet Junior School, London

Bob And His Hat!

Once, there lived a monster named Bob. He was a very good tap dancer. He had an emerald-green, shiny top hat and never danced without it. One day, Bob was getting ready for a show but he couldn't find his hat! He asked all the other dancers if they knew where it was, but none of them did. Sadly, Bob went onstage without a hat, until he saw it on the stage, waiting for him! Bob was so happy that he did the best dance ever and won the Nobel Prize ten times!

Liana Abdrabou (10)
Dulwich Hamlet Junior School, London

The Monster Under The Bed

Matilda saw a monster under the bed, he told her his name was Fred. Fred was blue and red, he had a brother called Ted. Fred could teleport. Ted had to be defeated, so they went to the airport. They caught a plane and went to Spain. They caught Ted in the act of stealing someone's mail. Matilda and Fred phoned the police and Ted went to jail. For a prize, Fred got a bike to pedal and Matilda got a medal, and as for Ted, he'd made his bed.

Thea Scurry (7)
Dulwich Hamlet Junior School, London

Emotions

Tom was an ordinary boy, but he had a secret. If anyone made him have strong emotions he would turn into a winged, hairy beast. That's why he had to avoid turning into that hairy beast. A mean and horrible kid named Zie wound him up in the toilets. Suddenly, he turned into the beast and flew Zie to the top of a flat. Tom calmed down, turned into the beast and flew back down. They became friends and never told anyone about it.

Arthur Pelser (8)
Dulwich Hamlet Junior School, London

The Monster Mash

One day, Dude woke up and went to school. He was playing with his friends. Death came up to him and he hurt him. Then, the next day, his mum came into the school and said that there was bad behaviour. Then the teacher said if they carried on then he would be kicked out for life. So then Dude walked home happily and Death had gone to Potty Club.

Hugh Carroll (8)
Dulwich Hamlet Junior School, London

The Lonely Monster

Once, there lived a monster and he was very lonely. So he went through many countries to find a friend, then he found a very mean friend, so he said no, so he found a very strict friend and said no, and finally he found a very calm and peaceful friend and he said yes and became best friends forever.

Dylan Hamilton (8)
Dulwich Hamlet Junior School, London

The Lonely Monster

Once upon a time, there was a boy. The boy was scared of the dark. Once, when it was dark, he looked under his bed and saw a monster. He was very scared, but... the monster came out and said, "Will you be my friend?"
The boy said, "Yes."
So they became friends.

Florence Decesare (8)
Dulwich Hamlet Junior School, London

The Lonely Dragon

One day, a little girl was woken up by a horrible noise.

"Mum!" shouted Layla.

"Yes?" asked Layla's mum.

"I hear something loud."

"It's okay," said Layla's mum.

"Okay, I'll go make breakfast."

At the volcano, a dragon was there, spreading fire all over, but they looked very lonely. There was nobody up on the volcano to play with, so she decided to make some friends, she went to a small house and went inside. She felt like nobody was home, but then she saw a girl.

Flame said, "Hi."

But Layla screamed.

Flame said, "I'm sorry, please be my friend! I am very lonely"

"Okay."

Kimberley Stewart (10)

Dyce School, Dyce

Bonkey And Bonkers

From a spaceship crawled two monsters. One was called Bonkey, the other Bonkers. They were from Planet Bonk. It looked like they were arguing. Bonkey was crying and Bonkers was being horrible to Bonkey.

"The journey home is going to take a while," said Bonkey.

"I don't want to go home!" said Bonkers, annoyingly.

"We have to try to fix the spaceship," argued Bonkey.

"*Fine, home it is!*" shouted Bonkers.

They worked for hours and hours on end. Bonkers was still angry.

"Two more parts to go," said Bonkey, happily.

After a few more hours, they were done.

"Woohoo, home!"

Eilidh Ross (9)
Dyce School, Dyce

Dr Scream's Mission To Save The World

He screams from a nightmare. "Argh!"
The scream wakes Sergeant Pigsly. He's destroyed half the population already. Dr Scream gets gear on. His house collapses. He's already given up but remembers what he's fighting for. He screams as loud as he can. "Argh!"
Sergeant Piglsy's knocked back. He gets a super-jump-potion and jumps up to him. He punches him to space and back but he comes back, even though he's so weak. He ends up on the ground and says, "I will be back."
Everyone's back, the town's rebuilt, everybody's happy. He needs a good night's sleep because he's tired.

AJ Stratton (9)
Dyce School, Dyce

Windy's Magical World

"Weeee! Ooh, what's that thing over there?" said Windy as she flicked the light on.

"Argh!" screamed Lucy. "Who are you?"

"Oh, hello! I am here to take you on an adventure," said Windy as she clicked her fingers.

Suddenly, they were in a magical world.

"Wow, this is so cool, how did you do that?" said Lucy, very confused.

"Oh, it doesn't matter, just enjoy yourself. Oh no, it's going to start raining! Wait, I know."

Click! Suddenly it was so sunny and Lucy walked around the magical world. But then it was time, so she went poof, gone!

Summer Taylor (9)

Dyce School, Dyce

The Defeat Of The Bad Lemonade Monster

Lemoner was swimming in the Lemonade Sea, then another lemonade monster came. Lemoner said, "Oh no!"

The bad lemonade monster said, "Hello, let's conquer the sea."

Lemoner was so smart. He said, "Okay," but Lemoner was lying.

Then they went attacking all of the other sea castles. There were only five castles in the sea. After invading four castles, there was only one castle left. They were going to invade the last castle but Lemoner pushed the bad lemonade monster to the beach, then the bad lemonade monster disappeared forever, so everyone started liking Lemoner. Lemoner was the king forever.

Ali Faruk Kahraman (9)
Dyce School, Dyce

Let's All Be Friends

In a school of monsters, Chub and Chubet were playing together. Chubet realised that Bubbles was sad, so she went to see if he was okay. Chub was sad now. He didn't like Bubbles. Chubet came over with Bubbles.

"Hi," said Bubbles.

Chubet said, "I know you don't like Bubbles but you need to get along with each other."

So they started to play together and it was working.

Chub said, "Stop! Bubbles, do you want to be friends?"

"Of course I do," said Bubbles.

Chubet said, "I told you you two would be friends."

"You did, now we're friends."

Lois Henderson (9)
Dyce School, Dyce

Football Adventure

I woke up and I saw a monster downstairs. He told me his name was Tongue because he had a long tongue. All he wanted to do was play football. I let Tongue play football for a bit. I told Tongue to come back in.

"Hate is here!"

Tongue asked me, "Who is Hate?"

I said, "He is a bad person, just use your power to fight him."

Tongue asked, "What power?"

So I said, "Your power shot."

"Oh," said Tongue. "I will save us! Attack! Okay, I am back, let's have a party! Hip, hip, hooray!"

Jamie Hopkins (9)
Dyce School, Dyce

Looking For Food

There were eighteen Cankocs but there was no food. One Cankoc felt brave, so he went looking for berries. Then he saw a small forest. Then he saw a big, blue monster covered with berries.
He said, "Come with me please, my family is hungry!"
So we fought the snake. Well, he fought the snake. We walked home together.
"To the desert, we go!"
But then I was snatched by an eagle.
"Help!" I said.
He grabbed me and punched the eagle in its face and it flew away. I went home with lots of berries. My family ate.

Franciszek Munro (10)
Dyce School, Dyce

Fire Vs Ice

The Flame Ship crashes on Planet Hot 'N' Cold. Firey and his crew are ready to fight but it's colder than Planet Toasty Roasty. He can hear the shivering of his crewmates as Icey approaches. Even though it's cold, they still need to fight. *Boom!* The fight has begun. Firey's crew are dodging the ice arrows and Icey's are dodging the fire arrows. Loads of Icey's crew are melting and loads of Firey's crew have frozen, so now it's just Firey vs Icey. Icey has run out of ammo and because of that Firey wins yet again.

Lucy Duff (9)
Dyce School, Dyce

Speedo Vs Chomp

Speedo was zooming through the sea like always when a meteor hit. Inside was Chomp. He was Speedo's worst enemy. He took all the fish! And Speedo! He took Speedo to Planet Age. He said, "Get ready to fight."
Three hours later, the fight began. The two monsters started to fight. It was a tough fight. Chomp lost one of his eyes and gills, Speedo lost one of his heads, but luckily Speedo's head regenerated and Chomp also regenerated and the battle continued. It was a good fight and Speedo won. He took all the fish back to Planet Earth.

Jack Masson (9)
Dyce School, Dyce

The Missing Wings

Bang! There was a portal. Buttercup went through it. She landed in a vast desert. The portal closed behind her, then she found a big cave. She went inside it and accidentally hit a button. *Boom!* She lost her wings, so she went on a big mission to find them. So she found some friends and they helped her. They searched everywhere, the cactus, the sand, and everything in the desert, but they couldn't find them. Then something magical happened, she got her wings back because of the teamwork they put into it, then she went back to China.

Anuthy Amothen (9)
Dyce School, Dyce

The Sad But Happy Monster

Mycky woke up from his BFF, Axy, calling him. Mycky did not pick up. So Mycky got ready for his day. He went to a restaurant for his lunch. When he walked into the restaurant, everybody... *screamed!* They ran out, even the waiters screamed. Mycky looked at himself and thought, *am I that scary?* He cried, sitting on the floor. "Why do I have to be so ugly?" he said with a sad face on.

Then he saw it on the news, the headline read: 'Ugly Monster'. Then his friend, Axy, called him and reminded him he was nice.

Flynn McKimmie (9)
Dyce School, Dyce

The Mystery Of Collin

One day, there was a big crash! A spaceship crashed on the Earth. A monster came out. "Hello there, my name is Collin. I'm from the Clums-o-planet," he said. "I wonder how I got here?"
I shouted, "How on *Earth?* My dream came true!"
We found out how he got here and I took him to the park. We met my friends there and we played 'park tag'. We played a couple of games and then... we had a quick party! Then the spaceship cake back and it took Collin! We felt sad and we hoped he would come back.

Lena Lubiarz (9)
Dyce School, Dyce

The Birthday Bomber

One day, I woke up to see a monster.
"Argh!"
I jumped out of my bed.
The monster said, "Do you want to help my birthday be the best?"
"Oh yes," I said.
So I got changed and he took me to Planetfluff. When we got there, the Fluff Hall where his birthday was, it was wrecked. We had to fix it, so we had all the monsters gather together. We stood there until someone admitted to it, about three hours later. Jeff, one of the monsters, admitted it and everyone came down to the hall and we fixed it.

Logan Skinner (10)
Dyce School, Dyce

The Little Monster

Up on a cliff, above a village, lived a small, pink monster named Fluffy. She loved to dance, and one day, a dance for monsters came. She really wanted to go, but she was scared she would get squashed. One day, she left her home and went. When she arrived, the gang of monsters who bullied her came over. They had nearly squashed her when a bigger monster came over. He stopped them and they ran away. After he had gone, Fluffy started dancing, it felt really good and nobody squashed her. She was good after all, she loved dancing.

Alexander Scott (10)
Dyce School, Dyce

Harry The Sky Monster

I woke up in the morning and looked under my bed. There was a monster. It had purple eyes and big ears. He rolled out from under the bed. The monster jumped on my shoulder. He said, "I can fly but I am losing my power."

So I took him to the vet. The vet didn't know what it was so I took him home.

I asked my mum, "Can I keep it? Please? Until he gets well. Please, please?"

"Yes."

It got worse so I took him back to the vet. He said he'd lost his power. Poor monster.

Quinn Hewitt (9)
Dyce School, Dyce

The Story Of Flame

In Lava Land, there was a leader called Flame. But he had an enemy. It was a peaceful day, but then the Water King invaded the Flame Village. But Flame had a plan. He built up all his power and sent out a big fire beam and so did the Water King. They fought and fought until the Water King got tired, so he stopped then left. Everyone loved him so, so much and they rebuilt the whole village, and the Water King was never seen again. Everyone praised Flame. The townspeople brought gifts like gems and jewels and diamonds.

Orla Thomson (9)
Dyce School, Dyce

The Monster From Mars

A monster called Spicky lived on Mars. One day, he woke up and he teleported. He was very confused, but then he teleported to an unknown planet. It looked different to Mars, he was very shocked. But then there was something that looked different to him, he didn't know what to do. He went to sleep because he was tired. But when he woke up he was somewhere else and something else too, but he was nice. At that point there was a noise, it was an alien. He fought him. They punched and kicked him, then Spicky won.

Logan Allan (9)
Dyce School, Dyce

The Universal War

Once upon a time, in the core of the sun, he was born. The Origin. One day, the Origin was strolling beside the sea, until... *splash!* Out of the water came Axy the axolotl. Eye to eye, and then... *boom! Whack! Bam!* The Origin charged up his ball of light and threw it at Axy. Axy used his water lash at the Origin but he blocked it with a sunbeam. They charged up their most powerful attacks and then both woke up, fighting for their lives... until they remembered they were the best of friends.

Calvin Cormack (9)
Dyce School, Dyce

Candy Land Story

There was a boy called Bill, he was a nice boy. He grabbed a glass of water and heard a bang in his room. He ran in to find a monster in his closet, he screamed but Fury told him to stop. The monster said he needed help to get to his home. Bill said, "Okay."

A monster appeared that looked like the other monster called Fury Ball, but the evil one, which was huge and called Evil Fury Ball. They fought as a new monster called Fluffy came to help Evil Fury Ball. Once they gave up, Fury left.

Mark Griffiths (9)

Dyce School, Dyce

Fun In Space

Cutie Pie was just about to open the fridge when her favourite shoe went flying into space, and she flew after it but it landed on a star. She was allergic to stars! So she found a really long space stick, got as close as she could and *she got it!* Then she went home and put the shoe in the fridge and went to bed, went under her covers and fell asleep. The next day, she had breakfast. Do you know what she had? Of course, she ate the shoe. Do you know what it tasted like? Salmon sushi.

Blaire Robertson (9)
Dyce School, Dyce

Daisy And The Hot Air Balloon

There was once a little elf named Daisy and she loved hot air balloons. Her dad was the chief elf and her birthday was soon, so for her birthday, her dad was going to get her one. A few days later, it was Daisy's birthday and the hot air balloon was there and they were blowing it up, but it had a hole! So Daisy went to the shop and bought some fabric, then she went home and sewed it on the balloon, but it was magic fabric and it granted wishes, so now Daisy could wish to go anywhere!

Saphia Clement (9)
Dyce School, Dyce

Dr Binox

There once was a lonely monster living in the sewers, and one day a big wave washed the monster away. He ended up in the middle of a road. He went to a forest to find a safe place to stay. He found a little cottage and people inside! He found a little boy playing in the forest, he went to go and meet him. The boy, called Alex, was frightened when he saw him, but he wanted to keep him and he called him Dr Binox. They were happy together and the parents were completely fine with it too.

Matthew Allen (9)
Dyce School, Dyce

The One And Only Gizmo Cat

As I woke up, I saw a... cat? I was confused, but I kept it. When I picked Gizmo up I got teleported. Then Gizmo left me. I packed my bag and left. I gathered Lily, my best friend, and Luke of course. I had my team. I went to the massive castle but there were none of Lord Dog's guards. As we got closer, there were more guards inside. We snuck into the castle and we found Lord Dog sitting on his throne. He pulled out his sword, but we had Luke and we ended up defeating Lord Dog.

Amy Weir (9)
Dyce School, Dyce

The Adventures Of Blob!

One day, I woke up and I looked under my bed and I saw a tiny blob.

I said, "Hi!"

He didn't respond. I took him out and he went huge. Nearly the size of my room. Then I named him Blob. I took him to see Hotel Transylvania at the cinema because there's a blob. I think he really liked it, so he went huge. I had to apologise to the other people... We went to get supper. I gave Blob blue sweets. We went home and I made a bed for Blob and we went to sleep.

Sofia Wells (9)
Dyce School, Dyce

The Disaster

When he called his best friend, Mycky, on Facetime, he fell into a portal. He felt dizzy, but when he fell out he was scared. But then he found his friend, Mycky, and he showed him around New York. But he saw his enemy, the Orgine, but he ignored him. But he found a man in a black suit, but when he showed his face, it was the Orgine. But he wanted to be friends and Axy said, "Okay." And they became best friends. The group was the Orgine, Axy and Mycky.

Rion Watson (9)
Dyce School, Dyce

The Pet Of The Shiba Ghost

Yesterday, I got a pet Shiba Inu. When my family went to sleep my dog went to a party. After she came back, we fed her, then she became a bit see-through. Then we went on a walk, but we couldn't put on her collar. So we went on a walk without her collar. When we came back, our dog was a... *ghost!* We sent her back to the pet shop but she escaped from the pet shop. So until this day, she wanders in the forest, haunting other people and animals.

Olivia Labus (9)
Dyce School, Dyce

Tim, Ben And The UFO Engine

Tim crashed on Earth and broke his UFO in the park and lost the engine. A boy called Ben was playing in the park and went home with it and used it for a project for school, it was a moving dog. Tim was seven centimetres tall and very bad and liked to steal lots of junk to make a new engine to go back home, but he wanted to make friends. Ben went back to the park to give it back, but Tim was done with the engine and then they were friends.

Katie Murray (9)
Dyce School, Dyce

A New Pixie

Up in the sky, Pixie was in her bed when she heard a sound. A little girl was on her cloud, so she played with the little girl and had some food and a milkshake and played dress-up, then went back to bed.

She woke up, had breakfast and did some baking, then more baking, when her friend came back to her cloud and played more games.

Abigail Dowding (9)

Dyce School, Dyce

Sad Monster

Once, when I was tidying my room, I checked under my bed and I found my toy monster. I brought him to the shop with me. All the people were laughing at the monster. When I got back to the house and my toy talked to me I thought I was going crazy.
The monster said, "No, don't say that, I am crazy!"
The monster said, "My name is Slimy. I love rabbits, cats and lots of animals."
I said, "Are you talking?"
He said, "Yes."
The monster told me that he never had a friend or family.
"I'm sad..."

Rosha Mohammadi (8)
Fane Street Primary School, Belfast

My Ginormously Huge Extraordinary Life

One day I went to the pet shop with my mother, trying to get a fluffy animal such as a bunny or a cat because we liked fluffy creatures. Then we found this small, cute animal and we really wanted to get it, so we did. We got a cage and all the necessities for the creature.

The shopkeeper said, "He really likes art, so take this art pad and this canvas," and we did.

We went home. I played with him and named him Baloney. He's actually very nice and kind.

"Yippee!" I said to myself, jumping with joy.

Ahmed Ahmed (9)
Fane Street Primary School, Belfast

Fuzzy Tries To Run Away

Something was under my bed, something fuzzy like a cuddly teddy. There were rolling noises like a bowling ball was gonna hit the bed. Slowly, a fuzzy, red ball crawled out from the bed, it had four arms and two legs, then ran out the door. Fuzzy rolled down the stairs and hid under the sofa in the living room. Then Fuzzy had a problem, he was just a ball and the front door was locked and he couldn't reach the door handle. He was too small, so he jumped but he still couldn't reach. He went crazy, bouncing everywhere.

Kieran Jiang (9)
Fane Street Primary School, Belfast

Thunder Guy And Mysterious Witch

One day, my monster wish came true. About six buddies, but two buddies were missing. Six-Eyes took them. He was my monster's enemy, he also had buddies. They were so small, like mine. They were so, so, so mean. I do not know why. Three hours later, I found a map leading to the missing two buddies. It said to go to Thunder HQ in the Thunder Academy. I'd been there before, it was amazing, but why would they be there? It was so dangerous unless Six-Eyes took them there on purpose. It took me three hours to save them.

Dylan McConville (9)
Fane Street Primary School, Belfast

The Lost Sisters - Part Two

Giggles finally found me but she still needed the key to unlock my cage.

"Finally, I found you!" shouted Giggles.

"Finally," Sqwigels said, worriedly.

"Okay, now we need to find Thorn. Oh wait, first I need to find the key," said Giggles.

"Okay, just hurry up," said Sqwigels, scared.

"Okay, I've got the key!"

"Yay!"

"But can we go home now?" said Sqwigels.

"No, not now."

"But why?"

"Because look," said Giggles. "T-t-the villains are here! Run!" shouted Giggles.

"But I can't," said Sqwigels.

I'm still in this stupid, smelly, rotten, stinky, bumpy, slimy, spotty, blunt, ugly, egg-smelling cage...

Verity Nicholson (9)

Godstone Primary & Nursery School, Godstone

Magnuss' Roller-Coaster Journey

There is a monster named Magnuss. He is a mud monster and can shape-shift, but right now he is travelling to find Mud-Man.

"Haha, look at this freak."

"Leave me *alone* Celsie!"

"Alright Magnuss, jeez!"

And that's Celsie, one of his enemies. As Magnuss walks off on his journey, Celsie and Mr-Cheese-Watsits, another bully, come strolling along.

"Magnuss, we are really sorry that we teased you," exclaims Celsie.

"Friends?" replies Mr-Cheese-Watsits.

"Of course."

"Hop on!" said Magnuss as he shape-shifts into a really fast car.

Vroom! As they arrive to meet Mud-Man, Magnuss is crowned as his Loyal Servant.

Merry Thackray (10)
Godstone Primary & Nursery School, Godstone

The Lost Sisters - Part Three

"Okay, now let's run!" shouted Giggles.

"Argh!" Sqwigels and Giggles screamed.

A day later...

"We should go find Thorn now," said Giggles, jumpingly.

"Okay!" said Sqwigels.

So we travelled the ocean, the desert, we went through a village and then we found a snowy mountain, and we knew that Thorn loved Snow. We started to look around, but nothing!

Suddenly (after four hours), we found another snowy mountain and we saw wings pop out of a cave in the mountain.

"I know those types of wings, they're Thorn's wings!" shouted Sqwigels.

"Who's there? S-sisters?" said Thorn...

Jess Young (10)
Godstone Primary & Nursery School, Godstone

Brookville Disaster

Magnum decided to travel, so he went to Brooksville, a long way away from Monsterville. He arrived at Brookshigh and the children were shocked! Trembling with fear, the children ran away.

After a while, they came back. The children hugged Magnum and snuggled him. Suddenly, there was a big roar and the children screamed with fear.

Huge, monstrous creatures stomped to the school. And then...

"We meet again, Magnum," roared the monsters.

"Oh no, it's Terror, Tink and Tumble," Magnum muttered under his breath.

They fought and Magnum shape-shifted to catch them. He is now the mighty hero of Brooksville.

Francesca Roberts (10)

Godstone Primary & Nursery School, Godstone

The Fight For The Dragon's Power

Long ago, a monster called Slimy lived in a different dimension. There was an evil sorcerer, the two-headed dragon. I was creating an invention, a portal, to find the dragon.

"Yes, I've made it."

"It's time to go in."

An hour later, there he was. I grabbed armour and a sword from dead soldiers who previously tried to defeat him. I was in a castle, so I swung from the drawbridge chain, striking him with my sword. He was dead.

"Where's his power?" Slimy said.

"Oh, of course, his heart," I replied.

It contained all of the powers ever known.

Antonio Pini (10)

Godstone Primary & Nursery School, Godstone

Lost Muggles

One morning, a monster named Muggles decided to go on a walk because he was bored. When he was on his walk, he couldn't find the path back home...

"Oh no," sobbed Muggles, "I've gone through the barrier."

After hours of walking, he bumped into a girl named Amy.

"Argh!" screamed Amy, as her dog, Sugar, barked along.

"Woof, woof!" barked Sugar.

"What are you?" asked Amy.

"I'm a monster and my name is Muggles," replied Muggles. "Could you help me get back home?"

"Umm... sure," said Amy in shock.

Millie Hoare-Simpson (10)

Godstone Primary & Nursery School, Godstone

Googly The Stinky Monster

Zoey and Jack are lost in a moving garbage can.

"I'm scared," said Zoey.

"We have to hide," said Jack.

Zoey and Jack tried to hide but they got caught by Googly the Stinky Monster. Zoey and Jack got stinked.

Googly said, "Clean people should go down!"

Googly went to stink lots of people and things got worse. Suddenly, Moonlight came.

"You are going down. Any last words?" shouted Moonlight.

"No!" said Googly, then Googly disappeared forever.

Now the world will be clean and healthy, all thanks to Moonlight.

Beritan Buyukertas (10)

Godstone Primary & Nursery School, Godstone

The Mission Of Moonlight

Once, in 2022, there was a monster called Moonlight, or Colour Monster. Moonlight was from Heaven and Hell because she could change her appearance by mood. Moonlight's mission was to kill the Stinky Monster, Googly. Googly was a monster that tried to stink humans. He tried to stink two people called Zoey and Jack, but Moonlight caught him and said, "Caught you, mister," put some colour on him that stuck him to the wall and strangled Googly.

That didn't kill him, so she took Googly to Hell and kept him there for all eternity so nobody has a stink spell.

Jessica Biggs (10)
Godstone Primary & Nursery School, Godstone

Oscar's Pizza Quest

Once, there was a monster called Oscar, he had a special power: he could shoot pizzas from his paw. One day, his enemy, horrible Bruno, crept up on poor Oscar and made him jump!
Bruno shouted, "I have turned out the power to the whole city!"
Oscar cried, "Fine, I will save the city."
Oscar set off on a quest to save the day!
After packing, he set off, nervous and worried. Well, once he stepped out of the door! He slowly went out of the door. He went to save the wonderful pizza city!
"Be back soon!"

Lois Spencer (10)
Godstone Primary & Nursery School, Godstone

The Lost Sisters - Part One

"Hi, I'm Giggles, the funny one."

"Hey," shouted Sqwigels and Thorn (my sisters). One day, Thorn vanished and me and Sqwigels were not the same. Then we saw a slimy trail of monster slime. But then I couldn't see Sqwigels anymore. Suddenly I fell down a trapdoor.

"Now I must find my sisters. I'll go to Sqwigels first," I whispered to myself, "because she is the youngest."

I had to get out of here, *like now!* I found a torch and then it got blown out by the whistling wind...

Evie Bradley (9)
Godstone Primary & Nursery School, Godstone

Octo Spider Saves The World

One day, a boy named Jack was playing Fortnite. Whilst walking home, he lost track of where he was going and ended up in the most deadliest forest. As he was walking he bumped into a bright tall white man.

"Hi, my name is Octo Spider, what's yours?"

"Argh! It's a monster!"

Jack started to run, but Octo Spider was faster. Octo Spider picked Jack up and killed him! He killed him because Jack was planning to take over the world and kill everybody except his crush, as he wanted them to be the only people on Earth.

Eleanor Scott (10)
Godstone Primary & Nursery School, Godstone

The Underground Bunker

It all started when one day after school, Amelia went to the park with her friends. Suddenly, a mysterious portal opened and something came out... something colourful and it looked worried. It all happened so fast, nobody saw it go in Amelia's school bag. When Amelia opened her bag to get her homework out... "Argh!" A monstrous-looking thing popped out! She stuffed it back in her bag and went to school. She forgot it was in her bag! It popped out, jumped high and ran. His name was Poot.

I wonder what will happen next...

Amelia Bateman (10)
Godstone Primary & Nursery School, Godstone

The Great Escape

There once lived a little, walking egg who was living his best life, but suddenly an intruder sliced the door down with a giant, thick axe. The intruder grabbed and kidnapped the egg, then put him in a giant frying pan and tried to cook him. Unexpectedly, his eyes turned black and he became evil. He made his way out of the pan with his razor-sharp teeth. Rapidly, he ran out of the house and finally saw the world, but he wanted more crime. Then, he started to make trouble with his awesome partner, Stretchface and sidekick, Donut.

Joshua Farrow (10)
Godstone Primary & Nursery School, Godstone

Monster Rumor

Monocropig was stuck in an abandoned village. Rumours said that whenever someone went to this monster, they would disappear.

The next day, the monster was featured on the news. A reporter went to the monster. The rumour might be true. The reporter was never seen again. When someone got to the monster its ears would catch fire and that happened quite often.

Uh-oh! It has just set a house on fire. After, the king of England decided to go to the monster. He went around the village and then went to the monster. Oh...

Riley Snashfold (10)

Godstone Primary & Nursery School, Godstone

The Villains Return

A long time ago, there was an ancient land named Monsterland. Now, let me introduce you to the villains Bad Egg, Stretchface and Donut, and the good monsters Giggles, Sqwigels and Thorn. One day, the goodies were solving a maths equation when... *Ring! Ring!* The bell went, it was time for playtime in the daisy field, when the villains walked in, turning all the daisies red and black. Suddenly, a solar eclipse gobbled up all the monsters! How will they escape the evil Bad Egg, Stretchface and Donut? And will they return?

Izzy Mosley (10)
Godstone Primary & Nursery School, Godstone

Blobby And The Mysterious Potion

One day, a monster called Blobby found a rocket. Five. Four. Three. Two. One. Blast-off. The rocket blasted off and it landed on a planet called Zepho. When Blobby got out, he saw a massive, shining light. Blobby thought to himself, *let's set out to find that light*. Two hours later, Blobby heard the laugh of his enemies, Darth Blober and Darth Mablob. As soon as Blobby heard it, he ran for his life. When he stopped, he was in front of the light and it was a potion. He drank it and he went to find his enemies...

Noah Austin (9)
Godstone Primary & Nursery School, Godstone

The Pibby Fight For Freedom

We were ready... then it appeared, the Glitch. It started fighting us. We tried our hardest and did it. But out of the Glitch, the big enemies appeared. They slammed us over and over but ultimately we did it. It was gone for now. Then out of the blue, another glitch appeared. Once again, we fought for hours.

Then three more glitch's appeared. We got one but still had three more to go, They're down. Two to go. It was getting harder and harder. Three down, one to go. I did the final hit and we won for now...

Alexander Mathews (9)

Godstone Primary & Nursery School, Godstone

The Electric Car Destroyer

Bobbat was in the scrapyard cutting up electric cars. Suddenly, he set the scrapyard on fire and drove off. The police chased after him. He rammed their electric police cars into trees to get away. Bobbat turned into a monster and went back to the scrapyard. He found an injured person and wanted to help him. He took him to the hospital. Bobbat went to fill up his fuel but later realised he didn't have a fuel tank. He drove off really fast. He thought, *I am an electric car!* Suddenly, he exploded.

Ollie Chiappa (9)
Godstone Primary & Nursery School, Godstone

Lexi's Lemonade

Once, there was a monster called Lexi who could shoot lemons out of her mouth. One day, she was venturing out of her home and she found herself at a village. Everyone was scared of her until she made a lemonade stand called Sparkly Lemonade. A human was brave enough to go and buy a glass, the monster was full of joy. The next day, the human told everyone the monster was funny and she had the best lemonade. Ever since she has been loved and built her own lemonade shop. Now all species of monsters are welcome.

Alannah Sheehan (10)

Godstone Primary & Nursery School, Godstone

Planet Bong

Far, far away on a planet nobody knew (Planet Bong) lived a monster called Victor. His mum (Frannah) too.

One day, he fell off his planet and fell to Earth and landed on Buckingham Palace. On his way, he bumped into a girl named Evie N-G and they decided to become friends. They did everything together, but one day, Victor decided to go home! "No!"

Evie begged and begged Victor to stay, so he stayed. They had a perfect time too and had lots of fun.

Evie Norman (9)
Godstone Primary & Nursery School, Godstone

The Among Us Battle!

One day the crewmates were doing their tasks. Suddenly, the imposter came and killed a crewmate. Then it came down to the imposter and the very last crewmate. They fought till the death and the imposter won.

Finally, they went to the next round and he became the crewmate. But then it glitched and turned into an imposter. He killed crewmate number 123. He went to the records and sabotaged the comms. He killed in the comms and won again.

Jacob Crozier (9)

Godstone Primary & Nursery School, Godstone

The Lost Monster

In the morning, Fred woke up to knocking on his window. It was a little monster with small horns with snowflake patterns on them and big friendly eyes. "Hello," chirped the strange monster.
"Who are you?" asked Fred.
"I'm the emotion monster. I need help," he chirped. "Follow me."
Fred followed the little monster until he saw a spaceship crashed in the woods.
"How can I help?" asked Fred.
"I need human DNA," said the monster. He grabbed his hand and put it on the spaceship. In an instant, the monster's spaceship flew away. Fred waved as the monster disappeared.

Riley Demirtas (11)
Gorebridge Primary School, Gorebridge

Flebble Turns Evil

At noon, lightning struck the top of the Eiffel Tower. Smoke blew through the wind as a strange essence awoke, emerging from the top.

A strange teal egg was left before me. The egg had been severely damaged from the strike. I never realised it was hatching until a tiny fluff ball awoke. She told me her name was Flebble and her flaming phoenix wings were more fascinating than anything I had ever seen.

She was so playful until I said, "Fruit Loops." *Bang!* Instantaneously she paralysed me and revealed her master plan to hypnotise everyone into her slaves...

David Simpson (11)
Gorebridge Primary School, Gorebridge

The Happy Monster

This story starts with a monster called Joy. Joy was a happy monster but one day Joy crashed and fell on Finlay's door. Joy knocked on the door and Finlay said, "What are you?"

Joy said, "I'm a Happycin from the planet Happy. I crashed and I need to get home."

Finlay and Joy went to see if Finlay had anything to help. "Maybe we could use bottle rockets," said Finlay.

"Yes, good idea," Joy said. He put cola bottles, some wings, parachute fins and... *boom!* Later, Joy made it back to the planet Happy.

Finlay Phillips (11)
Gorebridge Primary School, Gorebridge

Hello And Goodbye

One night a loud crash woke me up. I was scared but after a minute I peeked under my bed and a big slimy green monster was there. After a minute, the thing started to sign so it must have been deaf. It signed: 'I'm an alien'. I nearly screamed.

"We must get you home," I said with a grin. So I got out a book about how to make a rocket shoot into the sky. After deciding which ship, we started to build.

After hours of work, the monster signed goodbye and flew far away in his ship.

Sam Jameson (11)
Gorebridge Primary School, Gorebridge

My Bonkers Monster

One frosty night, I was fast asleep, but all of a sudden I heard a loud scream from my neighbour's house, then I heard a bang! I went over to investigate. The door was open. I walked in and I could hear feet scurrying across the floorboards and hard breathing but it was just Scream Bean the monster in one of his nightmares... "Going to the Hibs game?"

Me and Scream Bean are going to the Hibs game today. They are against Hearts. We are taking the train. I can't wait!

Aaron K (11)
Gorebridge Primary School, Gorebridge

Munchie

Once when I was going to McDonald's this pink fluffy thing shot right into my Happy Meal. I opened my box and the pink thing ate my messy salty chicken nuggets. I took her home and then took all the small crumbs of chicken nugget batter from her fur. I named her Munchie.

I took her to McDonald's once a week as a treat then I let her friend Cherry come round for Munchie's 3rd birthday. Cherry went home then me and my bonkers monster watched a movie called Monsters, Inc.

Kaitlyn Black (11)
Gorebridge Primary School, Gorebridge

The Story Of Bubbly

On a thunderous night, there was a girl named Skye who had a pet named Bubbly. They both loved football so they decided to go the next day again. But this monster we are talking about has soft yellow fur and bright blue eyes.

As they woke up bright and early they began to get ready to go to the football match. When they arrived there they got into their seats and watched the game.

The team they supported won. It got dark so they went back home and went to bed, *zzz*.

Skye Stevenson (11)
Gorebridge Primary School, Gorebridge

The Lost Toy

"Under the bench I found Dobby!"
"He's from Dobby Land, how did he get here?"
"A couple of days ago he lost his toy."
"Wait a minute, where is your toy now Dobby?"
"I dunno?"
"Did Big Dobby take it again?"
"I dunno."
"Will you stop saying 'I dunno'!"
"I dunno?"
"Shut up!"
The other day, Dobby found Big Dobby.
Dobby said, "Will you give me my toy back?"
Big Dobby said, "No."
"But please Big Dobby, that was my best toy. I used to bring it into school, remember."
Big Dobby thought.
"Okay then."
They were friends forever!

Phoebe Green (8)
High Green Primary School, High Green

Cookie's Cookies

It was a wonderful day in Dessert Land, until Cookie heard a scream. It was vegetables. Horrible, gross vegetables and they had strawberry shortcake.

"Oh no," said Cookie's pet.

No one else was here to save her but us.

"Get the exploding cookie bombs," said Cookie, "and fast!"

"Yummy!"

"No, we can't eat them, we throw them like this."

Boom! Boom!

And everyone was saved.

Then they said, "We should have a party in honour of Cookie."

But Cookie said, "Noo, that was not the end of the vegetables!"

Isabelle Gamban (7)

High Green Primary School, High Green

The Great Escape

I looked under my bed. I saw... monsters. Their names were Sunflower and Freder. I said, "Hello." They said, "Do you want to be on our team?" I said, "Yes." They said, "Hurry, hurry." The plan was to turn people back to normal. We went outside. We lived in a haunted house. We went outside. *Zap! Zap! Zap! Zap! Zap! Zap! Zap!* We did it! It was time to go home. "I'll see you around I hope. We'll leave you a letter every night and we'll meet you every night. Bye for now!"

Frank Parkinson (7)
High Green Primary School, High Green

The Missing Astronaut

Pies was watching TV about space. On TV she found out about a missing astronaut. She was determined to find this astronaut. So she built a rocket out of wood, pipes and metal. She set off in her rocket. It took her hours. She searched all the planets and she didn't find anything.

Then, when she was on the moon, she heard someone say, "Please, someone help me, please." She found him and got a ladder from her rocket. He climbed out and said, "Thank you so much." They both climbed into their rockets happily and set off home.

Georgiana Webster (7)
High Green Primary School, High Green

Liv's Lost Cat

Once upon a time, there was a girl called Liv. Liv woke up and her cat, Pearl, was gone. She saw some paw marks on the mud in her back garden, so she followed them and they led her to the enchanted forest where the Bogert Monster was tying Pearl to a tree. Suddenly, a pink and blue dragon appeared.

"My name is Flora," she said.

So she scared the Bogert Monster away.

"Thank you," said Liv.

Liv took Pearl home. She cuddled Pearl. They were so, so tired that they went straight to bed. They lived happily ever after.

Sophia Stupple (8)
High Green Primary School, High Green

Midnight's Bone

One morning, Midnight woke up and noticed her toy bone was missing! She looked all around her room, then she heard a noise from the balcony. She looked and Zenny was there with her toy bone. Midnight said, "Give me my toy back!"

But he didn't give it back to her. So they started to fight for hours, then Zenny gave up and he gave Midnight her bone back. When Midnight was playing with her bone, Zenny came and asked if we could be friends, and Midnight said, "Yes!"

So every day they played at the park all the time.

Imogen Eeles (8)
High Green Primary School, High Green

The Lost Toy

One morning, Wonka woke up and his toy was gone! He searched everywhere, he just couldn't find it. I heard an odd noise coming from the basement.

"*Hiss!*"

I trembled in fear... it was a snake with Wonka's toy! I went to karate and learned a move. It was kinda hard, tricky. I asked Wonka to wink when I could go. He winked and off I went with a thud and an oof! I got it back!

I was amazed and so happy! Wonka played with his toy all morning. I said, "Get to bed and have a brilliant, fantastic dream!"

Georgia Streets (8)
High Green Primary School, High Green

The Takeover

It was a great day until Smithy the enemy walked into Smyths Toys Superstores and tried to take over the toy store. Then he found Mr Smith, then they started a war. Mr Smith got his army. Then Smithy got his minions and started fighting. Mr Smith knocked all the minions down then started fighting Smithy, and Mr Smith used his powers and then defeated Smithy with a laser robot and he saved the day. All the toys bounced on Smithy and cheered. They all hugged Mr Smith and he was the hero of Smyths Toys Superstores, woohoo!

Layla Hill (8)
High Green Primary School, High Green

Where's Banana Frizz Gone?

It was a sunny day until Silly Banana Fudge the enemy came and took Banana Frizz into his lair. Then Silly Banana Fudge erased his brain so he could put him in chains, then walked out with his slave who put him in the chains. Then, when Silly Banana Fudge came back, his slave took Banana Frizz out of the chains so they could have a fight. Then Silly Banana Fudge lost, he was devastated. After, the enemy let him go. Then Banana Frizz walked home at 5pm in the afternoon. He could just see his house in the distance.

Elsie Richardson (7)

High Green Primary School, High Green

Billy's Adventures

Under my bed lived Billy. He lived in Gravity Falls, originally his enemy was Dr Pepper, he could do a backflip. He tried to defeat Dr Pepper. He did a backflip kick, it didn't work. He tried to do his iceballs, it didn't work too. He tried to get help but no one tried to help him. He was scared. He tried to help him, it didn't work too. He tried to do a mega kick. He did a mega punch, it didn't work too. He did fireballs, it worked! He was paid 10,000 gold, yay!

Casey Cottam (7)
High Green Primary School, High Green

Bob, Cob, Spob

One day I went to town. Once I was in town, I saw a monster. The monster had three heads and it was blue, yellow, green and red.

Then I said to it, "Where have you come from?"

It said, "We have come from Planet Three Heads and crashed on your planet."

After, I said, "You poor thing, let's have a party."

At the party, we danced and ate cake. Then it was home time.

I said, "Goodbye."

When I got home, I read my favourite book. I saw my monster waving at me.

Maeve Platts (6)
Kingston St Mary CE (VC) Primary School, Kingston St Mary

Spooky Monster

One day, I was watching a spooky film and a fat, green monster appeared. He said his name was Cookies. I was super scared. We watched some films together. Just as I turned, he wasn't there. I looked everywhere and he wasn't there. I kept thinking, *where could he be?* I called Mum but she didn't look the same. She had blue feet and square eyes, everything was weird. All the walls were covered in plants, the table was purple with spots, all the cats had spots, it was weird. I turned into a monster!

William Sweeting (7)
Kingston St Mary CE (VC) Primary School, Kingston St Mary

The Old Monster Book

One day I was reading my old monster book when suddenly a fluffy, hairy, cute monster with fifteen claws popped out. I asked her to play with me.
She said, "Yes, I will play with you or we can read a monster book."
"What is your name?" I asked.
"My name is Pib."
Then we had tea together on my bed. For our tea, we had sausages, mashed potatoes and peas, and for our pudding, we had doughnuts, sweets and chocolate. Finally, Pib and I went into the smooth bed.

Edith House (7)
Kingston St Mary CE (VC) Primary School, Kingston St Mary

The Book Of Monsters

One day, I was reading my favourite book when suddenly a spiky, three-eyed monster popped out of the book! Then I was scared.
It said, "Hi."
I asked if he wanted to play and he said yes, and he told me his name. It was Peamcuny. Peamcuny and I read a book, played board games and then I said goodbye to Peamcuny. So he jumped back into the book. And then I closed the book. I was down in the dumps because Peamcuny had gone home, so I told my mummy, so she checked my books for the monster.

Harry Bewes (7)
Kingston St Mary CE (VC) Primary School, Kingston St Mary

The Bouncing Pumpkin

I looked under my bed and saw an eight-winged pumpkin monster called Squashy (who was also cute!). We were always friends, she stayed under my bed all day but at night we played together, until the other night... We were playing hide-and-seek and Squashy was hiding under my bed and bouncing up and down. Suddenly, there was a major crash (luckily mum and dad weren't there). I had to think fast! It took me almost fifteen hours to rebuild my bed, but with the help of Squashy, the job was done in no time.

Clara O'Keeffe (6)

Kingston St Mary CE (VC) Primary School, Kingston St Mary

The Strange Animal...

Last week I went to the amazing zoo. In the zoo, I saw a strange, spiky, red and black creature. It was a monster! I slowly thought that I should take him home, so I did. On the way, I got spiked on the shoulder! Finally, we were home, but when I looked back he was gone! That night I looked everywhere but he was nowhere...

When it was bedtime, I heard a small snoring sound. It was the monster. I was so happy! "Where were you?" I asked. But he did not answer, only a small shriek.

Jake Ewing (7)
Kingston St Mary CE (VC) Primary School, Kingston St Mary

Blob Finds A New Home

One day, Blob crash-landed in Africa and he met some lions and some cheetahs. Blob played with the lions and the cheetahs. Blob met some parrots, they were red and blue. Then Blob found a town and he made a friend and then they played all day. In the morning, they had hoops for breakfast. After breakfast, I saw lightning hit a tree. Then the fire started! Blob rushed to the river and absorbed all the water. He came back and put the fire out. Blob went to his new home and fell fast asleep!

Jack Gray (7)
Kingston St Mary CE (VC) Primary School, Kingston St Mary

Fluffy Monster

One day, I was eating candyfloss and a scary monster popped out of the candyfloss. It was fluffy, silly, pink and blue. Her name was Fluffy and she was adorable. I was excited to see her and we played a game of hide-and-seek. It was the best day ever. So we played and played, then mum saw the monster. Mum loved Fluffy monster. Me, Mum and Fluffy monster played a game of tag. Then we got thirsty and we got hungry. We had Oasis and sweets. We watched TV and fell asleep until morning.

Dolly-Rae Sharland (6)
Kingston St Mary CE (VC) Primary School, Kingston St Mary

Block

One day, I was watching TV and there was a bang on the creaky door. I went to open the door, I saw the biggest monster ever. It had lots of heads, a long body and long arms. The heads were black, the eyes were black and everything was black. It was the scariest thing I had ever seen. We went to the park and played on the luscious, green, twirly grass. I scored a goal. He was a rubbish goalkeeper. It was one-nil. I was getting happy. I asked him what his name was, it was Block.

Alex Parkinson (7)
Kingston St Mary CE (VC) Primary School, Kingston St Mary

Blood Monster

One day, there was a monster in the living room. I saw him under the couch. He came towards me with his blood-red eyes, one tooth and a book. Then it sucked me into the book and I landed in Monster World. My monster told me his name was Blood. There were so many rides but I wanted to go on the Ferris wheel. Blood took me to the top of the wheel but it broke down! Blood jumped down and used his mind powers to stop me from rolling away. Then the monster sent me back home.

Jacob Glynn (7)
Kingston St Mary CE (VC) Primary School, Kingston St Mary

The Book Of Monsters

Last night I opened my Book of Monsters when suddenly, on the first page, there was a monster with five ears and three eyes. It appeared on my bed. I closed my book but the monster was still on my bed, so I said hello and it said hello back. Also, I told my mum but she would not believe me. We played on the Nintendo Switch, had a hot chocolate and we watched the sun go down, counted the stars and had a cuddle. I opened my Book of Monsters and the monster went in.

Sophia Tompkins (6)
Kingston St Mary CE (VC) Primary School, Kingston St Mary

Red Hedge Koala In Hug City

Last week I went to Hug City and I met a cute monster. I slowly thought about taking them home. We bought some popcorn and sweets on the way home. When we got home, we played some video games on TV. Then we played with my toy after we played with my dog. Then we went to the park for a bit and we did some gymnastics. After we met Will, my best friend, and we went to the movies to watch Sing 2. Then he gave me a big hug, then he disappeared.

Phoebe Cann (6)
Kingston St Mary CE (VC) Primary School, Kingston St Mary

Hops

One sunny day, I was in the garden when suddenly I heard something on the swing. It was a brown rabbit with a horn, scars on its cheek, a giant carrot, a second head, blood on its tooth and red shoes.

"Do you want to play with me?"

It said, "Yes!"

We did gymnastics and roly-polies! Then we went to the park and we went to bed.

Connie Mace (7)
Kingston St Mary CE (VC) Primary School, Kingston St Mary

The Jumping Monster

One rainy day, I played a fun game and a massive, hairy monster jumped on me and he was a spiky monster. I quickly hid him behind the sofa because my mum and dad came into the room. I quickly turned the TV on and sat down very fast and they went out of the room. I looked behind the sofa and I looked outside the window and he was jumping on the trampoline.

Stanley Hartnell (7)
Kingston St Mary CE (VC) Primary School, Kingston St Mary

Scarlett And The Pink Monster

One day, when I was reading my favourite book about monsters, suddenly a strange egg appeared. The egg started to crack, then a cute, pink monster started to lick me. I started to giggle. Soon, the monster started to cry because she was hungry. I started to feed it with creamy milk. When the monster was finished we played amazing puzzles about monsters.

Scarlett Goretzka (7)
Kingston St Mary CE (VC) Primary School, Kingston St Mary

Rex

One day I was out in my shiny fishing boat. I went down the stairs and saw a slimy monster. I didn't know what to do! The slimy monster followed me up the steps. Suddenly, I heard a blood-curdling scream. It was the monster scraping his foot on the step. He told me that he was banished from his world and needed help...

Hunter Forrest
Kingston St Mary CE (VC) Primary School, Kingston St Mary

The Monster In The Forest

Last week, I went to the forest because I was walking my dog, and suddenly a monster jumped out of a prickly bush and made me jump. My dog ran away. He chased me and my dog all the way home but I noticed that it was asking for help. I helped the monster and we became friends. For lunch, we had hot chocolate and sandwiches.

Sasha Peckitt (7)
Kingston St Mary CE (VC) Primary School, Kingston St Mary

The Evil Monster

One day, I was doing my jobs when I spotted a monster! He had spikes all over and was very vicious... I ran and told the guard but the guards couldn't stop him! A little while later, he broke into Area 51 to try to free his family... But they got captured and transported to the most secure prison in the world!

Harry Morgan (7)
Kingston St Mary CE (VC) Primary School, Kingston St Mary

Red Devil

One scary night, my mum took me to bed. When my mum switched the light off, my Red Devil Play-Doh came alive. It had blood-red horns. It jumped on my bed, I almost fainted. We played tag and Lego and hide-and-seek. I heard my mum so I said goodbye.

Charlie Hull (7)
Kingston St Mary CE (VC) Primary School, Kingston St Mary

The Farting Competition

Farting Eyes was going to a competition. "Oh goody," said the monster, "I'm very excited." When he opened his mouth a butterfly went inside. *Gulp!* He farted. "Oh yes, I'm totally going to win and get new friends," said Farting Eyes.

The next day, Farting Eyes came to the stage but suddenly his farting powers disappeared. When it was his turn, he tried with all of his might and came a big, green cloud that grew behind him. Everyone put pegs on their noses and he won! "Congrats!" everyone clapped. He got more friends and won a farting cup!

Bushra Ahmed (7)

Moorland Primary School, Beanhill

The Lonely Monster

Once upon a time in the bright forest lived a monster called Bella. She had no friends because she had no powers.

"I need some friends!" she said as she ran into the dark forest.

Then a scary creature lurked towards her. Bella really loved art so she quickly made a flashlight. There were three amazing monsters there. *Should I be their friends?* she thought.

"Can-can we be friends?"

And the monsters nodded... Suddenly, the ground was shaking, it was an earthquake! Then Bella made a hut. Sadly, Bella and her friends were never seen again.

Ella Ogunkoya (7)
Moorland Primary School, Beanhill

The Trash

"Wow! A portal."

I slowly walked through and landed on a roof? I went into a class and started to trash everything! Children went outside, screaming, "Help!"

I found a bin, I just glued it for no reason, made a frame on the wall and put the bin on it. I think it's pretty! I went to hide as the children came and saw the bin! They looked amazed. As I climbed the roof and went sadly into the portal, suddenly a big party!

"For me?"

"Yes, you," said Mr Fries.

I took everything and carried on with the party.

Anna Rzepecka (9)
Moorland Primary School, Beanhill

My Monster Friends

Once upon a time in the jungle forest, there was a lonely monster called Spots who wanted to make friends. The next morning, Spot flew down to Planet Earth to make friends with humans. Spots knocked on the man's door but it didn't work at all because she sounded just like a fox. The next morning after that didn't work either because the women didn't understand what Spot was saying. The next morning, Spot hid behind a tree, crying. In the afternoon, a crowd of animals formed a circle then hugged her. The morning sun shone then Spot's friends hugged.

Olivia DeRoche (8)
Moorland Primary School, Beanhill

Food Crash

Walking by the shops, Charity was so good at balancing food on her head. She was always praised by people. But there was someone watching. The person was called Miracle the bully. Charity was walking by the shops with lots of food. Miracle jumped out and all the food splatted everywhere on the planet. Everyone came to the council and thought.

Charity said, "We could eat all the food on the planet."

Everyone said it was a good idea, so they tried. Soon, all the food was cleared up. Everyone cheered for Charity and even Miracle the bully did too!

Fatimah Abdul Kader (8)
Moorland Primary School, Beanhill

Crazy Hair

"Help! Crazy Hair is going to people's land because no one is in her land, what can we do?"
She went to people's land and everyone was looking at her. Someone called the police on her, what could she do? When she went to her house and placed her rainbow handbag on the table, suddenly a hair potion dropped onto her feet and her hair started to grow long.
"Oh no!" she said.
Until the police came and arrested her. In a blink of an eye, the hair tied them up.
She smiled and she lived happily ever after.

Janice Zira (8)
Moorland Primary School, Beanhill

Star Wars: The Story Of Baby Yoda And The Mandalorian

He was a cute little furry thing, he looked like the opposite of the devil. He would help anyone and anything, even the most untrusted person in Star Wars. He once tried looking for the Mandalorian but he couldn't see him anywhere, so he smelled for DNA. He found some, travelled as far as he could go and smelled the scent of a lost friend. The scents were everywhere around him like he was underground. A few seconds later, he saw a figure in the distance. It was the Mandalorian and he was captured. He leapt quickly, then... *boom!*

Dexter Mardel (10)
Moorland Primary School, Beanhill

Thornkill And The King Of Blooukins

One day in Jupiter's jungle, Thornkill was feasting on Blooukins, not knowing his mortal enemy, Glofin, was setting up a trap. As Thornkill ate, he fell into the trap, not having an idea of what would happen. The next day, he was on Earth in a zoo! Then he remembered Glofin, also known as The King of Blooukins. He'd trapped him on Earth. Five days had passed. He lost it. He lashed out, destroying the zoo. As he'd destroyed the zoo, he realised his enemy had trapped him here. He knew where he was... he travelled and died!

Reuben Greenall (10)
Moorland Primary School, Beanhill

The Red Devil Strikes Again!

The game was here, the final, 0-2 down against Liverpool. The Mighty Red scored two. Suddenly here's number 222, the Golden Devil! The Red Devil passed it to the Golden Devil. He scored, 1-2 against Liverpool! The pressure was on, 1-2 at Old Trafford. The Liverpool player Mighty Red injured the Red Devil. He got back up, it was a free-kick. The Red Devil scored, 2-2. The Mighty Red and the Red Devil were fighting. The Red Devil used fire to send him to Mars. Two minutes left, 2-2. It was a tie. The Red Devil scored. Man U won!

Kya Durman (10)

Moorland Primary School, Beanhill

Siren Head

One day, Siren Head was walking in the city, smashing cars. But people thought he was a bad monster.

So the news said, "There's a bad monster in town so stay in your houses."

He was so mad that he started smashing buildings and hurting people. But there was a ten-year-old boy saying stop it and he was the only human outside the house. He was so happy, he stopped smashing things. That was Siren Head's best friend. But he was sad that he smashed stuff, so he left forever and never came back from town.

Quincy Zira (10)
Moorland Primary School, Beanhill

The Monster Park

One morning, a spotty monster was on his own planet, playing in the monster park. He was playing on the big, red slide when suddenly it broke. Sam went on the monster swings. But it was tiny, so he got stuck. Next, he went on the roundabout and he fell and hit his head. He had to go to the monster hospital.

The people said, "You can go home."

He went home and went to bed. The next day, he went back to the monster park and fixed the swing, the slide and the roundabout because he was kind.

Connor Lacey (7)
Moorland Primary School, Beanhill

Mrs Stockton And The Messy Monster

One dark day, Mrs Stockton found a rock. But it wasn't a rock! Suddenly, it hatched and a monster popped out. She had twenty pink eyes and a huge face. There were fourteen arms on her pink body. After, they got some paint, then they walked to Moorland Primary School and put the paint on their feet and ran around and made a mess in every classroom.

Suddenly, Miss Trofa came with Miss Gargan and they said, "That is not what we do."

They helped them clean and never made a mess again.

Sumayyah Kigozi (7)

Moorland Primary School, Beanhill

Daniel's Bonkers Monster

One day, Daniel saw a shell but it wasn't a shell! It was an egg. It hatched! It was a Bonkers Monster. It was a tiny, friendly and smiley monster. He went to the park with Daniel. They were playing catch. Suddenly, the ball went far away. The monster went after it and got lost. Daniel found the monster. Daniel was so happy. Daniel hugged the monster. He was happy to see Daniel! Daniel took the monster to the funfair. They played happily and then the monster ran away! He was never seen again.

Hassan Naqvi (6)
Moorland Primary School, Beanhill

Muchmun Goes To France

One day, Muchmun decided to go to France. She went on a plane. It took ages. Finally, she got there. She wanted to go to the Eiffel Tower. Then she went to a hotel. She stayed for five days. Then she went back to Scotland. She came home to see them but her parents were not there. She began to cry.
She shouted, "Mummy!" but they didn't come. Then there was a knock on the door. It was her mum.

Dara Olorode (6)
Moorland Primary School, Beanhill

Peaca Boo Goes To Leeds

One day she was very bored.

She asked her mum, "Can I go to Leeds please?"

She said yes and she started to walk. Peaca Boo was very happy to go to Leeds and she was the happiest monster in the world. Her mum was a bit worried and scared because she was going to Leeds.

Her mum shouted, "Come back right now!" and she still walked and walked! She saw a dinosaur and she shouted loud!

Isla Bickerdike (6)

Moorland Primary School, Beanhill

Joshua And The Cinema

Once, there was a monster called Joshua. He went to the cinema and he kicked everyone out of the cinema. He had a party at the cinema. Then he played football and kicked the ball so high that he made a hole in the cinema. Then he did some horse riding in the cinema. He had so much fun inside the cinema.
His mum said, "It's time to go home."

Ruth Boakye (6)
Moorland Primary School, Beanhill

Oli The Monster Going To His Granny's

One day, Oli went to his granny's to have breakfast and his mum came with him to have breakfast too. Then they went back home and went to bed. The next morning, he went to the beach and then he went to school and he did good work and went home and had dinner. Then he went to bed and the next morning, he had breakfast and went to school.

Oli Patton (6)
Moorland Primary School, Beanhill

Taco Flies To London

Taco likes football. Loves football. Arsenal play, their stadium is in London. He will fly to see them play. He and his friends want to watch the football on TV. Liverpool wins and Arsenal loses.
"No!" says Taco.

Destiny Edwards (11)
Moorland Primary School, Beanhill

Monster Missing

"Scrrr blah beemp?" asked baby Grogu.

"Okay, we can play tig," said Mando, "let's go!"

He halted.

"Where are my golden dentures?" Mando worriedly said.

Mando turned around.

"Where's Grogu? Ah, I know where he will be, catching frogs. Right, I better get there fast. Okay, I'm here."

Rustle, rustle! Bam, bam!

"Oh no, Luke Skywalker! Oh no, there's Grogu, he's in the muddy water. Not again," whispered Mando, "well, I'd get a tasty snack if I had my golden dentures."

The bounty hunter walked off. Mando picked Grogu up. Grogu smiled and in his mouth were Mando's golden dentures.

Lucy Antrobus
Our Lady Of Lourdes Catholic Primary School, Birkdale

The Starfish Robber

The sea town was silent except for a loud scream coming from Princess Mimi.

"*My crown is gone!*" she screamed.

"My darling, where is your crown?" asked King Triton.

"It's gone, Father. Someone took it!" sobbed Mimi.

"I will have to go and find it," she said, very determined.

"If you have to darling," sighed King Triton, sounding concerned.

"Bob!" exclaimed Mimi. "You have my crown!" she said as she spotted the crown. "Why did you take it?"

"Because I wanted to get attention," Bob said, shyly,

"Just ask! Anyway, let's be friends!"

Madison Fashoni (10)
Our Lady Of Lourdes Catholic Primary School, Birkdale

The Missing Golden Bonkis!

Bang! The confetti went everywhere. The crowd cheered but suddenly gasped as a terrible scream came through the crowd.

"My Golden Bonkis! They're gone!" cried Basher.

I glared at Sir Bonkilot who was smirking. Something was very wrong. I looked again and he was gone. Basher saw too and ran after him. As did I. I couldn't catch up though.

Sir Bonkilot cried, "How did you know it was me?"

"We guessed," Basher replied, "and we knew."

"Yes," I said, "you're going to Brushiland now! You are Bonkilot the thief, not sir!"

Luckily the Golden Bonkis are back! Yay!

Daisy Halfpenny (10)
Our Lady Of Lourdes Catholic Primary School, Birkdale

Happy Will Always Beat Evil

One day, Crazy was turning people happy when suddenly... *crash!* Something had crashed onto a building. So Crazy rushed to the building and found a monster.

Then Crazy asked, "What is your name?"

"My name is Evil, or you can call me Cold."

"Okay Cold, why are you here? Because I am on a mission to turn the entirety of Earth evil."

"Why!"

"Because I hate humans and the devil told me to."

"Okay."

In his mind, *challenge accepted*.

Cold went around turning people evil, but Crazy turned them back, and over time Cold left and Earth was saved.

Sean Porter (9)

Our Lady Of Lourdes Catholic Primary School, Birkdale

A Horse Named Cal!

One day in Shelby Stables, Cal and Bounty were grazing on grass in the paddock.
Then Bounty whispered, "You better sleep with one eye open."
Cal was scared. Then, one night... Cal went missing! Aubrey and Autumn looked everywhere. Then, the next morning, they saw Bounty was stepping on Cal! They pushed Bounty off when they realised. They put metal around his stable and moved him away from Cal.
The next day, Cal said to Bounty, "Don't kill me!"
Next morning, Bounty said to Cal, "Follow me... hehehe!"
Cal followed him. Bounty led him to a ditch. *Boom!* Cal fell...

Emilia Gregoriou (10)
Our Lady Of Lourdes Catholic Primary School, Birkdale

A Step Forward For Slayers

Muichiro the Mist Hashira encountered a fierce enemy. His name was Kokushibo. Muchiro was trembling but he had to fight. Their battle began, both using their breathing, but Muichiro was pinned to the wall. But lurking in the shadows, the Wind Pillar appeared, and the Stone Pillar, while Muichiro was healing. But then the upper one revealed his true form, it was ugly but strong. Suddenly, Kokushibo's body started to melt. He was dying. He remembered his brother, the reason he became a demon was to surpass him in strength.
He said to himself, "I'm truly sorry, my dear brother..."

Jack Higham (10)
Our Lady Of Lourdes Catholic Primary School, Birkdale

Billy Vs Purple Mosquitos!

It was just a normal Friday at school when our teacher, Miss Byrne, was doing some maths with us. *Bang!* We heard a loud crash outside and we all saw a battle against Billy and the Purple Mosquitos! Suddenly, our innocent teacher turned into a Purple Mosquito! After that, we all felt a little bit worried. Luckily, Mr French Man came through the door with his chip knife and killed all of the Purple Mosquitos, including Miss Byrne. Then Mr French Fries Man said, "My full name is Mr French Fries Man, have I not told you that before?"

Sienna Shawcroft (9)

Our Lady Of Lourdes Catholic Primary School, Birkdale

Just Because You Have No Talent Doesn't Mean No Friends!

"Hello, I'm Malteser, want to be friends?"
"Ew no, you have no skill, unlike the rest of us!"
Then Malteser walked off sadly. The next day, Malteser tried and tried and tried to find his skill, but it wouldn't come. He tried the slushy shop, no trick. Skatepark, no trick. But just then, he went to the hoverpark and he found his trick! His trick was riding on a hoverboard. After the weekend, he went to school proudly and everyone wanted to be his friend! He showed his tricks and now had lots and lots of friends!

Matilda Hunter-Wearing (9)

Our Lady Of Lourdes Catholic Primary School, Birkdale

Being A Monster To Being Nice

There was a little alien. The alien was born in an intergalactic zoo. Ants could only see how little aliens were so they tried to eat them, but aliens could grow quick. It took twenty days and then they were big. Unfortunately, 80% of aliens died from ants. Luckily, lots of ants were in cages so you could adopt them. Now 80% of aliens would not die. That one alien remembered that ants could kill aliens, so he started being a monster, killing ants.

Everyone said, "Stop killing the ants."

Then one human came and made him nice.

Noah Gavan (9)

Our Lady Of Lourdes Catholic Primary School, Birkdale

King Ghidora

King Ghidora and James were out fighting enemies. James went to fight enemies Noah and Isaac when Ghidora went to fight poachers. James was out of sight when swarms of poachers came with guns. They shot but Ghidora fought back and when it looked like the poachers were going to win, King Ghidora used a special ability that summoned lightning out of his wingtips. There were very few of them but more came, and when it looked bad, James came and killed them. Then they had a delicious dinner of Noah and Isaac and poacher dips and chicken.

Seve Arthur (10)
Our Lady Of Lourdes Catholic Primary School, Birkdale

The Warriors

One day, James and King Gidora found buildings broken and windows cracked. All you could hear were bombs from Isaac and Noah killing innocent people. Everyone was screaming, but James went to fight and kill Isaac and Noah. King Gidora went a separate way and went to kill poachers. As James was going to Isaac and Noah, a bunch of robots surrounded him. He thought he was doomed. Then, out of nowhere, King Gidora ate and bit all of the robots. James was really shocked and ate the last pieces of the robots that surrounded him.

Alfie Owens (9)
Our Lady Of Lourdes Catholic Primary School, Birkdale

Billy The Three-Headed Monster

There once was a three-headed monster named Billy. The three heads all had different minds so they could argue. They were all playing together when one of the heads hit another. All of a sudden, they were all arguing and shouting.

Then, suddenly one of the heads said, "Jksmlopqstuu," which meant, "Guys, we need to all stop arguing all of the time!" in Billy's language. They all realised how stupid they were being and all said sorry. They all became friends again and they were all happy.

Lily Friel (10)
Our Lady Of Lourdes Catholic Primary School, Birkdale

Shape Man's Stolen Eye

Shape Man lived on Planet Crazy. His enemies were aliens. One day, Shape Man's eye fell out! While Shape Man was looking for it, a naughty alien stole it! Shape Man saw and chased after it. After he couldn't anymore, Shape Man climbed up a ladder and saw the alien hideout. He ran but there were lasers as doors. Shape Man climbed up to the open kitchen window and sneaked into the safe room. He saw the eye and took it. Alien three saw him and chased him but Shape Man was too fast. He lived happily ever after!

Emilia Gorna (9)
Our Lady Of Lourdes Catholic Primary School, Birkdale

The Magic Of History

One day in icy Poland, Ella found a history book in her attic. She opened the book to a page on WWII. As quick as a flash, she was being warped into the page. Then she noticed she was in Poland in WWII. Suddenly, a monster called Anne appeared. They saw bombs dropping on people's houses. They quickly helped the people out of their houses and saved them. The people thanked them and smiled. Suddenly, Anne grabbed Ella by the sleeve and teleported her back to her attic. Ella was never more proud to be Polish.

Emma Moreno Gouveia (10)

Our Lady Of Lourdes Catholic Primary School, Birkdale

The Missing Swimming Suit

There once was a monster called Flapper that got a magic swimming suit for his birthday that could change anyone into a creature that lived underwater, or at the edges of the water. The next day, it was stolen by a human and they put it on and swam off in the sea! Flapper saw his fish friend in the sea and he asked to ride on her to chase after this mysterious human, she agreed! So off they went in their traveller. Eventually, they got the human and they took back the swimsuit and became the best BFFs.

Louisa Lunn-Bates (9)
Our Lady Of Lourdes Catholic Primary School, Birkdale

Egg And Friends

Once upon a time, there was an egg, his name was Egg. All of his friends kept getting stolen by all of those boastful humans. They ate all of his friends, the best looking ones first. How silly, you should always save the best till last. So Egg decided to make a super cannon blaster and all of the humans got knocked out and Egg escaped from the fridge. Egg found an eggbox and this was his brand new home that he decorated, and he also found himself some new egg friends.

Edward Halsall (10)
Our Lady Of Lourdes Catholic Primary School, Birkdale

The Monster Under Your Bed

"Good night," said Dad as he turned off the lights, "and don't let the bed bugs bite..." he whispered before closing the door.

Chase, who was curled under the blanket, was terrified of the dark. Sweat dripped down her head while her heart pounded. She took a peek from under the blanket and saw two red eyes peering at her. A pair of claws reached for her ankles.

"Help! A monster is under my bed! The Bed Beast is back!"

Dad rushed through the door and switched on the light.

"Don't be silly! There are no monsters under your bed!"

Rida Fathima (10)
Priory School, Slough

The Hunters' End!

Once upon a time, in the forest, there were hunters searching for a prisoner, but they found something else! A monster. One hunter touched the monster and boom, they exploded when he roared!
"I'll go to the city."
He went and the people were kind to him.
"Hide! The hunters are coming!"
But then *boom!* They were all on fire and ran. Fireshooter had a plan, he did it. Hunters came, they got a clear rocket launcher and Fireshooter blew his fire in the rocket and *poosh, boom!* The hunter army was gone and they lived happily ever after.

Eesa Khan (7)
Priory School, Slough

Escaping Professor Vizion

First, there was a monster called Nitwig. He was wandering around until he got kidnapped. The kidnapper wore a mask but couldn't breathe, so he took off the mask and he was evil Professor Vizion. He said, "Hello, Nitwig Broakufred."

Nitwig was shocked that he knew him and said his real name. Vizion brought Nitwig to his lab and said, "Welcome to my lab."

The lab was enormous, Nitwig escaped by fighting Vizion. Nitwig won but saw that Vizion felt sad that he lost so he gave Vizion a trophy. Vizion turned normal and Nitwig and Vizion became friends.

Zayn Ahmed (8)
Priory School, Slough

Lola's Adventures Through Time

Lola flew through the time machine and landed with a soft bump on the gravel. She looked around feeling dazed. Next, she stood up and took in her surroundings.

"Oi!" a man behind her exclaimed.

She turned around and saw that he was wearing a yellow hi-vis which said 'Police'. Lola ran faster than she had ever run before. Stumbling across another portal, Lola hurriedly started the long process to get it working. *Pow!* She had made it. Lola saw her parents running towards her and felt a wave of excitement flood through her. She was finally home.

Evie Prescott (9)
Priory School, Slough

The Crazy School Day

It was a normal day in Chesterfield High, Class Swarrington had a new, unusual teacher. He wore a bright, snappy suit to school and talked funny. He stuck pencils to his head and ate paper for fun. He was crazy! That day Swarrington was confused. The class asked what his name was.
He answered back funny and said, "Mr Gobble."
Soon it was clear Mr Gobble was not human. He ripped up books and climbed on tables!
"Is he okay?"
Later that day, Swarrington was informed that Mr Gobble was not human. In fact, he was a monster in disguise.

Mishika Ahluwa Lia (9)
Priory School, Slough

Alan And The Scientist

Once, there was a scientist who created experiments and technologies. One day, he accidentally made a wormhole and fell into it. He found himself on a different planet called Manoila. He bumped into a monster who was out jogging. The monster called Alan thought the scientist was an enemy - they got into a big argument. The scientist threw potions, one of which turned Alan's fur pink, which made Alan furious. After a few hours, they sat down exhausted and agreed to have a quiet battle of chess. They decided they quite liked each other and agreed to be best friends.

Ruby Gill (8)
Priory School, Slough

Friend In The Forest

Once upon a time, there was a monster named Little Buddy. His life was great except for one detail: he was lonely. But nobody wanted to be friends with him. One day, he was very sad. Another monster named Little Bella saw this and asked, "Why are you sad?"

The lonely monster told her the story. Little Bella told him she would be his friend and Little Buddy's world was happier, better, fuller. After that, Little Buddy and Little Bella became best friends. They were inseparable. They were like two small peas in a pod. They are still friends today.

Saiuri K Naidu (9)
Priory School, Slough

Scary - The Monster Who Lives On The Planet Mars

A long time ago, humans decided to go to Mars. They used a rocket ship to go to Mars. They crash-landed on the sea on Mars. They tried to fix the ship. Suddenly, one of the parts disappeared. There was a four-eyed monster, called Scary, behind the ship. The monster started fighting with humans. So humans used rocket parts to kill the monster. The humans destroyed one of Scary's eyes. All the humans ran around the sea to protect themselves from Scary. Then one person fell into the sea and found a glistening rock. He picked it up and it exploded!

Vihaan Panchal (7)
Priory School, Slough

Sunny's Skill Search

There once was a monster called Sunny, who was a kind, gentle girl. She was always happy but longed for a skill. One that would shock people, and it was then she decided she would search for one, and she did find one. Actually, lots! All fun that she loved and she soon realised her favourite skill was football. This small, furry monster had realised that if you believe in yourself, you can achieve almost anything you want. After she learned this, she never stopped and found lots of hobbies: singing, dancing, racing and many, many more to enjoy.

Nafisa Khan (9)
Priory School, Slough

Haunted Palace

One day, a monster entered a city called Paris. He tried to rule the amazing town called Viller. He then found a haunted house in Viller. He had smelled delicious children - yum, yum, yum. He growled and growled until everyone ran away. So he sneaked into the palace where the queen and king lived. He saw the queen's and king's children, so he chased them and he tried to eat them, and he did. When the queen, king and their children weren't alive, he would be able to rule Paris and the town called Viller especially and he became kind.

Yasmin Zekari-Day (10)
Priory School, Slough

Amy On Star

Once upon a time, there was a monster called Amy. She lived on Nova, an ice-cold planet, but one day there was a war with another planet called Miaral. The war was so big that Queen Amy's mother sent her to a different planet. Amy went to many till she found one that reminded her of her home planet, then she found one called Star. But then, ten years later, when she was eighteen, there was a war with the planet that destroyed her home planet. So she fought for days and days and they had won then they celebrated.

Esha Tandon (10)
Priory School, Slough

A Dream To Achieve!

Once upon a time, there was a monster called Spikey Dude and he loved cricket. His dream was to be a cricketer. But he thought it was easy to achieve his dream.

He was saying to himself, "When will I ever be a cricketer? I have to practise. But I don't have any bat or ball. So how will I practise? I could get some from the shop."

He found the perfect shop. They had everything he needed. He practised so well that he could go to a cricket stadium and then he got a shirt. He did it!

Abdullah Basit (7)
Priory School, Slough

Killer Kor

Jake, the boy who had no end to his curiousness, decided to not go home today. Playing with his friends, he saw a glimpse of an orb emitting green light inside of a dark, gloomy cave. The young boy was baited by the light and his senses told him to touch the orb. His heart skipped a beat and he was teleported to another dimension. He was there. Jake was staring at thousands of bones, sitting in a pile. Kor was there. Jack still had his lunch. He gave it to him and acted friendly. Kor was tamed.

Hasan Jawad (10)
Priory School, Slough

The Monster That Went On Holiday

Once upon a time, there lived a monster called Luca. Luca lived in the lovely, new woods. One day, his mum decided to go on holiday. She said it was going to be a Monster Resort. After that, they were driving there. When they got there, Bubbles, Luca's mum, showed Miss Mam the booking card. Miss Mam was the hotel owner. When Bubbles and Luca got into the room, it was a mess. But Luca had an idea!

"Let's tidy up the room," said Luca.

One hour later, the room was tidy. They went on amazing adventures.

Alana Chan (7)
Vita Et Pax Preparatory School, Southgate

Brayen Goes To The Beach

Once, there was a monster boy called Brayen. He liked to watch TV at home. One day, when he was watching TV, he became really bored, so he asked his mummy and daddy if he could go to the beach. When he got to the beach he went for a swim in the sea. He met a crab in the water and they became good friends. They made sandcastles together on the beach and played football and they shared a double cone ice cream with two flakes. They spent the whole day together and waved goodbye when it got dark.

Martyn Yavari (7)
Vita Et Pax Preparatory School, Southgate

The Magic Tree

Zig was running in the forest, he heard footsteps from behind him. He came across a tall tree with dangling vines. Zig saw mushrooms all around the tree. He was so hungry, he picked one and threw it in his mouth. His nose itched, his eyes began to sting and his legs felt weak. Zig saw his body begin to vanish. He felt a bit scared but he didn't need to hide anymore.

"Those mushrooms must be magic."

Being invisible meant he could find his way home safely.

Emilia Maestri (6)

Vita Et Pax Preparatory School, Southgate

Hugo The Monster's First Party

Hugo was excited to go to his friend Pedro's horse-riding party. When he arrived, they showed him the pony he was going to ride, it was called Daisy. Daisy the pony started to buck in the arena and Hugo got scared. Just before Hugo could scream, he was on the floor. Hugo was crying and the teacher came to check that he was okay. He wanted to be brave so he got back on the pony and enjoyed the rest of the party with his friends.

Francesca Spiteri (7)
Vita Et Pax Preparatory School, Southgate

Monster Picnic

Miny was a furry, little and kind monster. She lived in a tall, grey, black and white house, and Miny was purple. Miny liked picnics so she decided to go for one. She brought a cheese sandwich, apple, chocolate cake, a blanket and biscuits.

She met a bad monster that looked good and Miny said, "Hello."

The monster hit Miny. Miny taught the bad monster how to be good and then they had a picnic together.

Ellena Wilson (7)
Vita Et Pax Preparatory School, Southgate

Blub Blub And The Secret Tunnel

Once upon a time, Blub Blub crept into the gloomy tunnel. He could smell the delicious, sweet chocolate. There was a big party for the King Monster, Waca Waca. He had demanded eighty-eight balls of special chocolate slime, but the slime was gone. Blub Blub's sister had eaten it all. He spent all night making more. Poor Blub Blub.

Emily Strien (6)
Vita Et Pax Preparatory School, Southgate

Flying Dino Rockets

John flew his dino rocket to the starting line. He was going to race over 100 miles per hour to the moon. When the race started he was in third place. When you hit a magic moon rock it makes you go faster! The race was nearly over and John was in second place. He hit a magic moon rock and zoomed into first place. John had won!

Joseph Murphy (7)
Vita Et Pax Preparatory School, Southgate

The Day Duncan Left

One day, Duncan left his house. He was scared. He was going swimming at the pool. His new teacher was a human called Miss Hibberd. He was scared because humans have two eyes and Duncan had three eyes. But then he met Miss Hibberd and she was very nice.

Hannah Vallayil (5)
Vita Et Pax Preparatory School, Southgate

Young Writers Information

We hope you have enjoyed reading this book – and that you will continue to in the coming years.

If you're a young writer who enjoys reading and creative writing, or the parent of an enthusiastic poet or story writer, do visit our website **www.youngwriters.co.uk**. Here you will find free competitions, workshops and games, as well as recommended reads, a poetry glossary and our blog. There's lots to keep budding writers motivated to write!

If you would like to order further copies of this book, or any of our other titles, then please give us a call or order via your online account.

Young Writers
Remus House
Coltsfoot Drive
Peterborough
PE2 9BF
(01733) 890066
info@youngwriters.co.uk

Join in the conversation!
Tips, news, giveaways and much more!

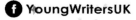

f YoungWritersUK   **🐦** YoungWritersCW   **📷** youngwriterscw